MT 44/24 FIC (CRIME) £3

COFFIN I

GWENDOLINE BUTLER

Praise For Gwendoline Butler

'Gwendoline Butler is excellent on the bizarre fantasies of other people's lives and on modern paranoia overlaying old secrets; and her plots have the rare ability to shock'

ANDREW TAYLOR, THE INDEPENDENT

'[Butler's] inventiveness never seems to flag; and the singular atmosphere of her books, compounded of jauntiness and menace, remains undiminished'

PATRICIA CRAIG, TLS

'Butler distils her own brand of disquiet: omnipresent and irresistible'

JOHN COLEMAN, THE SUNDAY TIMES

'The imaginary Second City of London... together with its well drawn characters, make this a quietly compelling read'

JOHN WELCOME

Gwendoline Butler

COFFIN FOLLOWING

CT Publishing

First published in Great Britain 1968

This edition 1999 CT Publishing.

Copyright © Gwendoline Butler 1968

The right of Gwendoline Butler to be identified as author of this work has been asserted by her in accordance with the Copyright, Designs & Patents Act 1988.

Editorial Consultant: John Kennedy Melling

All rights reserved. No part of this book may be reproduced, stored in or introduced into a retrieval system, or transmitted, in any form, or by any means (electronic, mechanical, photocopying, recording or otherwise) without the written permission of the publisher.

Any person who does any unauthorised act in relation to this publication may be liable to criminal prosecution and civil claims for damages. This book is sold subject to the condition that it shall not, by way of trade or otherwise, be lent, re-sold, hired out or otherwise circulated, without the publisher's prior consent, in any form or binding or cover other than in which it is published, and without similar conditions, including this condition being imposed on the subsequent publication.

A CIP catalogue record for this book is available from the British Library.

ISBN 1-902002-10-5

9 8 7 6 5 4 3 2 1

Book design and typography by DP Fact & Fiction

Printed and bound in Great Britain by Caledonian International Book Manufacturing, Bishopbriggs, Glasgow.

This book is fiction. All characters and incidents are entirely imaginary.

COFFIN FOLLOWING

Chapter 1

IN THE BEGINNING there was violence. A single act of bloody violence. First there was a blow, then a scream. No one heard the scream. But the scream went echoing on and on. And the blow, although it brought a terrible silence, did not bring quiet. No act of violence ever truly dies away; the effects of it go on forever.

In the crystal ball the old woman could see it. From the beginning to near the end. She was a genuine seer and although a lot of what she saw was rubbish some of it turned out to be true.

She saw John Coffin, whom she knew, on the run, and she saw three women and three acts of violence. She was fascinated. It was the best story she had ever seen. She watched the pictures appear, flow into each other and disappear. The girl or woman, girl really, seemed to be dead already, anyway she was stretched out white and still. So was the second. Or was it the first again? "Remarkable," said the old lady. The third woman appeared to be Coffin's wife, whom she had never liked.

"Oh, I wish I could see more," she exclaimed. Nothing was ever complete in her crystal, she never saw everything. The crown tilted crazily on her head and she put up a hand to steady it. She was practising wearing a crown again.

After some thought she reported what she had seen to the police. But her story did not convince them and they took no action.

Crystal balls were out of fashion that season in police headquarters.

The year when John Coffin was ill, the year of the crystal ball, was the year he decided to take himself in hand. After thirty-nine years in the world, a career, a marriage, some success and the usual amount of failure, there is bound to be some slack to be taken up. For John Coffin, policeman, living in his own manor in South-east London in this year of grace there seemed an uneasy amount. He had gone wrong somewhere within himself, he knew it and if he didn't do something about it very soon the world would know it. His wife knew it already. Perhaps it began with her. That was the sad thing, it might very well begin in their private struggle. Sometimes he thought there was too much of war where there should be love. That in itself was better and more hopeful than a vacuum, so all the knowledgeable said. He had tried, in this war's more painful moments, to appreciate this and say, yes, here is vitality and not death, but, reeling from individual blows, it was not easy to take in a general truth. But whether proceeding from this or not, there was something else wrong besides. He had begun to be convinced he was made of stuffing and some of the stuffing was seeping out.

The illness of course did not last for a year, only a few months, but by the time the whole process was over it felt like a year and more. It started with a bullet through the thigh and a concussion brought upon himself by momentarily taking his eyes off two men he was arresting. One man hit him and the other shot him, both were now in prison. But for John Coffin it had meant weeks in hospital. The bullet wound soon healed, but the effect of the concussion seemed to go on and on forever. Even after he was technically fit again, his memory seemed to come and go and his emotions went up and down like a seesaw. Also, he had headaches. And after the headaches he had insomnia. On his doctor's advice he took a solitary holiday in Italy, but so far from helping him the heat bored and exhausted him and he returned rather crosser than he went. Things were still not good at home.

And in addition to the headaches and the insomnia he had this strange strange illusion that he was dissipating into thin air, that every day there was less and less of him as a man. Sometimes he thought he was a straw man and his stuffing was coming out and other times he thought of it as a process of osmosis by which he was being gradually absorbed into the atmosphere. But whichever it was it was highly unpleasant.

It seemed better to bear it alone. He left his wife behind in their home and moved out to a bachelor flat near the police station which was his district headquarters. This naturally caused the maximum gossip and comment but fortunately he was too far gone to notice it.

"Do you think I am losing my reason?" he asked his doctor.

"Well, no, it's not as easy as that."

"Easy," groaned Coffin.

"Going mad is probably a lot nastier," said his doctor sympathetically.

"What's it all about then?"

"You've had a crack on the head, it's disorganised you a bit," he stopped.

"I've had some pretty peculiar thoughts."

"I don't think it's dragged anything to the surface that wasn't there underneath before," he said carefully.

They looked at each other.

And I won't come back and see you again for advice; that's today's peculiar thought for one, said Coffin to himself vindictively.

He was really shocked at the extremely unpleasing thoughts he seemed to have these days. It was as if he had been bottling these thoughts inside himself for years and now they had all got their hats on and were ready to come out.

"I don't think you're ready to go back on duty yet," said his doctor. "No." He said the last word rather quickly seeing the look that flashed across his patient's face. "Take a bit longer and really get yourself in order."

But Coffin could still control himself "Thanks," he said. "I think I'll do that." It seemed to him, at that moment, that there were a lot of things his memory had extruded, that they were now trying to get out and it was better to help them. "I think I'll do that," he repeated.

He was on long paid leave, and then unpaid leave. He had money but he gave most of it to his wife. Soon he began to be very poor. He moved to a cheaper room. He was living in a different world.

He thought no one was watching him, but of course plenty of people were watching him really. In the first place someone is always watching you in London and not always with such friendly eyes either, and secondly, there was the district itself.

The district he had moved into was a huddle of quite poor respectable houses near the river, not far off Pickle Herring Creek. It was a street of yellow brick houses, small and mean. Considering they were little houses you could keep extraordinary secrets in them.

The person who watched him most was the girl who had nothing to do but watch, the girl in the house opposite, the girl who lived in the room on the top floor.

She was a pretty girl with long fair hair and golden eyes. Pussycat pretty she had called herself once. She was rather a bedraggled little pussycat now. In spite of everything she was doing her best to keep herself clean, but it wasn't easy.

"Well, I'll tell you how it was," she said to herself She talked to herself a good deal nowadays, seeing that there was no one else to talk to. "I never meant to come to this house. I never meant to come at all."

Why had she come then? Why was she here? At the moment, it was a question she couldn't answer; she was still working it out. Perhaps she would find out one day. Indeed, she meant to. Meanwhile she watched John Coffin who did not know why he was where he was either.

From her little window she could see him sitting at a table. He spent a good deal of each day sitting at this table and she always wondered what he was doing. He might be reading, perhaps, but he didn't look as if he was reading. Perhaps he was table-turning, she thought one wild day when her thoughts had been whirling round more than ever. She giggled. She was surprised at being able to giggle. Who'd have thought a fragile thing like a giggle could survive what she had been through? But what had she been through? She had a memory, an impression, of having been through something, but it was getting increasingly difficult to pin it down. Memories shouldn't be like that. But her memory didn't seem to be at all what she'd been brought up to believe memories should be. In fact sometimes she had the distinct impression that her unpleasant experience was not something she had behind her but something she still had to look forward to, a promise and not memory at all. At these times her pulse began to leap and her mouth go dry.

"I never meant to come," she said again. "I shouldn't be here now." That's a fact, she thought. I shouldn't be here now, in this desolate empty room. Who should be here now? No one. That's who ought to be here in this empty room. It ought to be empty. "Those who don't mean to come shouldn't arrive," she said aloud solemnly. Still, she had arrived. And here she was.

"No, not table turning after all," she said, looking down at John Coffin. "He doesn't have his hands on the table." Not much of the table was within her view, just the edge, covered in a pale cloth. John Coffin's hands were folded in his lap. "Why, he's just thinking," she said. "He's sitting there just thinking."

So there they were, the two of them; one whose memory was not what it should have been, the other who had plenty of memory, all precisely labelled, and suddenly found every bundle was dirty and unpleasant to handle.

At this stage John Coffin hadn't noticed her and thought the house opposite was empty. So it was—empty. Practically empty. It had paper and paint on the walls and furniture in the rooms and even a little food in the cupboards but it was empty of people. In the evenings what life there was in the house opened up, but even then it was a poor subdued sort of life that showed itself only by the putting out of a milk bottle and the drawing of the curtains, which were never opened much anyway. *Someone* came home then, and that was about all you could say.

John Coffin didn't even attempt to say that. He let his landlady do all his saying for him. She told him what he would want for his supper and where the launderette was so he could wash his shirts. She told him often that she didn't want anyone in her house who wasn't clean, but she never offered him a bath. There *was* a bath. Coffin had seen it. A tin bath that lived in the garden and came in once a week. The rest of the week a big tomcat seemed to live in it.

It was true that he sat almost all the time at his table, but he wasn't just thinking (as the girl across the road had decided). Mostly he sat there reading, his hands in his lap, his book propped up in front of him. He wanted big books supported on piles of other books. He was reading anything and everything. He wanted to feel that his mind was being flooded with ideas and facts so that all his old systems of thought were swept away and his mind cleansed. That was why he wanted books in an endless supply. So that he could feel assured of a long enough read to get thoroughly washed.

His landlady called it drugging yourself with books.

She watched him on his daily trips to the free public library and wondered where he got the money to spend the whole day reading.

"I wonder if he drinks?" she asked herself, watching Coffin on his way out. He had three volumes of Balzac under his arm and was off for the next three. Anyone who drinks while reading Balzac is asking for suicide, but the name had meant nothing to her when she read it. Of course, she noticed what he was reading just as she would have studied his letters if he had had any. She used her literacy that far.

The girl in the house across the road looked down at Coffin as he passed. She waved her hand at him, hoping to attract his attention, but he did not look up. It was such a tiny wave through such a tiny area of window that you could hardly expect him to.

Coffin might have sensed something, though, because he shifted the books uneasily under his arm (Balzac was quite a weight) and looked up and down the street. There was nothing to see except the battered little houses and the empty road. In front of every house was an unemptied dustbin. Only once had the dustbins been emptied during Coffin's stay, but they seemed always standing there in hope. He kicked one as he passed. An empty beer-can rolled out and then another and then another. Embarrassed, Coffin picked them up and started shoving them back into the bin. Some beer dribbled out, down his sleeve and up his arm. He patted himself dry with his handkerchief.

In the library the girl assistant silently handed over the next three volumes of Balzac. She watched sceptically as he thanked her and walked out.

"There's twenty-four more to come," she called after him. "And when you've finished those you can start on Zola. He's the end of the alphabet, but you can go back after and try Proust."

Coffin turned round and looked at her, but did not answer so that she felt ashamed of herself. In fact he had not heard her. People often said things to him these days that simply floated over his head. Now he could see the words coming like bubbles out of her mouth but he had no idea what they said. Politely, he tried a few bubbles himself.

"Thank you for keeping the books for me."

"No one else wants them. There's no demand."

"No, I suppose not." He looked doubtfully at the books. "It depends how you feel, I suppose," he said, not telling her that the vigorous sturdy life he found in them was supporting him now. "There's a lot in it, of course. A good lot of reading, I mean. That's what I go for. I feel the need of a long book."

"Most people who come in ask for a short one. Don't give me anything too long, they say."

"We must be reading for different reasons."

But he had gone too far. She thought he was odd, her first reaction to him was intensified now, he was too much like the fiction he read, and she turned back to the shelves.

And Coffin went away angry that he who had once handled relationships like balls to knock about, now could not even talk to a girl about a book. *But you could not manage your relationship with your wife, could you?* asked a voice inside him.

Next door to the library was a clean humble shop

where you could drink coffee and milk and fruit juice and eat rolls and cheese. Coffin usually went in there after his visit to the library and drank coffee. He liked to sit at a table in the window if he could because it was a tiny table and he never had to share it with anyone. On the days he came and drank coffee here he never ate anything else until evening. He had to watch what money he spent. He hadn't exactly lost his sense of the value of money, but now it meant something different. Before, money had meant a holiday with his wife, something pretty for her to buy or wear, a pocketful of potential possessions. Now it simply meant so many more days in which he could afford to forget himself. If he lowered his standard of living still more he could go on affording this luxury even longer.

The shop was on the corner of the main road and the street where he lived was just around the corner again. It was a dusty and unlovely main road, full of small cheap shops selling clothes and shoes and hardware. Farther down the road was a covered market for meat and fruit and vegetables. They were near the docks here and all the produce was cheap and good. The housewives of the district knew what was what and had a keen idea that they wouldn't buy second-rate food. They pinched and picked and quarrelled over the food and told the stall-keeper what they thought of him and he told them back. Coffin observed it all in a remote amused kind of way, as if it was another world, very different from his old alert professional gaze. Distantly, he thought he recognised one or two faces. A fat man in a cloth cap who walked through the streets wearing a blue blazer and carrying a carpetbag full of shopping looked to him like an old friend he had put away in prison for five years for a robbery. And surely the thin postman who passed his house every morning was a member of the far-flung Dove family who numbered supporters both of the law and of crime in their enormous kindred. It was even rumoured they were bringing up a promising member as a lawyer, hoping to make him a barrister and place him on the Bench. No one doubted that if this was what the Doves wanted it would eventually be achieved. It might take one or two generations but they bred in tremendous numbers and could aim at any number of mutations. The girl who served the coffee in the dairy had a familiar look too and he thought he might have seen her somewhere. He recognised them but he hoped they didn't know him. He thought he had changed and that therefore they wouldn't know him.

"I seem to know that man, don't you?" said the girl who served the coffee.

"He's a copper," said the owner of the shop briefly.

"What's he doing round here then?"

"They say he's gone off his rocker."

"What, mad?"

"Sort of. Had some trouble or something. But I think that's just the cops covering up for one of themselves. If you ask me, he done something and they turned him out. They can be very nasty about one of their own that's slipped off the rails. But they don't like it talked about."

"You known him long?"

"Been around here for years." He turned back to his coffee machine. He had been very careful to keep in the background so that Coffin could not see his face. Their acquaintance had begun in a way he preferred not to have remembered, even by a broken-down copper. "Any of us might come to it, I suppose," he muttered to himself "I've gone up in the world and he's gone down. That's how it goes." He hummed quite cheerfully to himself as he watered the coffee.

A tall quick bright-eyed young girl walked up to the counter and asked for a glass of milk. She was an *habitueé* too and the assistant spoke to her at once.

"See that man you passed on the way in? He's a policeman."

"What, with all those books?"

"He's an ex now. Something wrong."

The girl drank her milk, leaning against the counter. She watched Coffin turn the corner and disappear. From where she stood she could see the office where she worked. It was a large welfare organisation, one of whose departments occupied itself with a search for missing relatives, daughters, sons, husbands and wives, fathers too. Mothers got lost relatively rarely. They tried, no one could say they didn't try, but they didn't often get away with it. They came back. There must be something in mother-love after all.

The girl, although her skinny white sweater and her tiny red and white skirt made her seem juvenile, was really an important member of the missing persons department.

"Even police forces have their throw-outs," she murmured.

She finished her milk and swung her black patent bag jauntily over her shoulder.

A beaten ex-policeman, she was thinking. He might be just what I need.

Quite unaware of her interest, not much warmed by his coffee, John Coffin walked home. He plodded on, head bent, eyes on the pavement. But he must have been a little more open to the world than he had been. Presently he looked up.

He had no idea what had made him raise his head. He stared about him, saw nothing more than a small grubby street and started to move on. This time, though, he didn't drop his head.

He walked head up. Then he stopped. Once again, out of the corner of his eye, he had caught sight of something. He stared, carefully focusing his gaze on what had attracted him. Strange, he could even use the word 'attract' inside himself, and yet the world had done nothing but repel for weeks past.

There it was again. A tiny movement at an upstairs window of the house across the street. It attracted. It was meant to attract. It was a wave.

He walked on, keeping his eyes on the window but trying not to think about the wave. A wave implies two people: the waver and the waved-at. Coffin didn't want to be the second. Also, a wave arouses questions. Such as: why wave?

I don't know anyone here, thought Coffin. Not to wave at. Then he added carefully to himself, "I mustn't be bitter about this. I'm still a human being."

There was a plump squalid man on the kerb looking into his dustbin. Or *a* dustbin. Perhaps it wasn't his own. He might just be interested in garbage. But no, it was a massive over-filled dustbin, it matched him.

"Here, what d'yer think," he said to Coffin. "I've lost my teeth in this here bin. They dropped out just as I was putting a bit of old rubbish in." He bared his gums at Coffin in proof. "I always knew they was too loose. I said so to the dentist. 'They're too loose,' I said. 'Better than too tight,' he said. 'That depends who's doing the biting,' I says." He was digging in the bin, shovelling away the rubbish like a large dog after a bone. "Well, I dunno where they've gone to."

"There's a girl up there waving," said Coffin, pointing to the house.

"No." He looked up briefly, shook his head and went back to his digging.

"There's a girl up there. I saw her."

"No. Course not. She's been dead thirteen years."

He seemed to have no more to say. Coffin looked at him blankly for a second and then walked on without a word. He looked up at the window but now he could see nothing.

He repressed the enormous surge of anger that made him want to rush back, shake the man and say: "Who's been dead thirteen years? There was a girl there, I tell you. I saw her."

He kept his eyes fixed on the window as he walked, but he saw absolutely nothing.

The house was directly opposite where he was staying; he stood staring up at it. If ever a house looked empty that one did. The old lace curtains at the window had the dirt of years on them. On the ground floor one broken window was boarded up and another had a piece of dirty flowered curtaining stretched across it.

There was an empty milk bottle on the front step which was a negative indication of life.

But Coffin knew that houses in London which looked as if they must be empty and ought to be pulled down did in fact have someone living in them. No. 14 Spicerman Street was not going to be an exception to this rule. And anyway, he had seen the girl.

He let himself into his temporary home. No key had been given to him, but you didn't need a key, at No. 13 Spicerman Street a key was kept on a bit of string hanging behind the letter-box and you pulled it through and let yourself in. As a policeman Coffin deplored the habit; for a lodger it had its uses. Avoiding his landlady was one. Another was that if you didn't own a key the sense of belonging to the house was minimal. I don't have a key, you could say, I'm a bird of passage, I don't belong. And that was how he wanted it.

Spicerman Street ran down to the river near where the clove and nutmeg carrying spice-ships had once come in, and once perhaps the spice warehouses had spread their pleasant smell over the area, but if so it had long since been defeated by the London air. The main smell at the moment was the smell of rubber. On the skyline were still the impressive outlines of a few huge eighteenth-century warehouses and in his more cheerful moods Coffin liked to think they still housed cloves and peppers.

The front door banged behind him again and his landlady entered the house with her shopping in a string bag. She was accompanied by a large black cat which was standing on its back paws trying to drag at something in the bag. Coffin sniffed. He could smell it as well as the cat; a very very ammoniac skate.

"Get down, Timmy, get away from me. Leave my supper be." Her voice was high. Timmy was a large battered cat with only one eye and that with a fierce red glow to it, and she was a tall gaunt plain woman. Of the two her lodger preferred Timmy. There was also a husband who was hardly ever seen. Coffin thought he worked down the old Spice Yards, but what he did was a mystery. He was not an attractive figure. Coffin imagined his wife didn't care very much for him, either, from the grim note in her voice when she spoke of him, and he rather thought they kept up the old custom of a fight every Saturday night.

Anyway, she seemed to have a bruise on her cheekbone now: and a cold in her nose, but that was permanent. Nearly twenty years of free medicine, thought Coffin, and she still hasn't got rid of her sniff. The smell of fish rose up and hit him in the face and he winced a little. He stepped backwards and trod on the cat, who swore loudly.

"That girl in the house across the road," he heard himself say in a loud voice. "Who is she?"

"What girl?" asked his landlady, giving the cat a kick. "I don't know about a girl."

"The girl across the road."

"There isn't one." She was searching the parcels in her bag, feeling them and counting them. Apparently she found what she wanted, for she nodded and let the bag swing free. The fish slid to the floor where the cat triumphantly found it.

"There is. I saw her."

"No. Hasn't been for years." She fought off the cat

and picked up the fish.

"I was watching her."

She was angry and suspicious at once. "Here! I don't want any of that in *my* house."

Coffin turned abruptly into his own room, shutting the door in her face and leaving both her and the cat standing together in the dark little hall.

She smelt the beer on his coat-sleeve and sniffed. "Been drinking," she said. "He's been drinking."

The girl across the road saw Coffin come in and take his usual seat by the window. She knew then that she'd had another failure of communication. It was terribly terribly hard to get through, as if there was a wall between her and the rest of the world.

She herself could see and hear well enough, but here too there were strange gaps and things came and went in the most amazing way. For instance, she didn't believe she lived on air, but what did she eat? She could remember a few meals, but the whole impression was blurred. Then what about sleep? Sometimes it seemed to her she must really be asleep the whole time, and everything a dream. Other times she felt as if she never slept at all.

She put a hand to her head. It ached. Surely that was real? She seemed to remember an accident that had been the cause of the ache, but as soon as the memory hinted that it might appear, it tantalisingly disappeared again.

But now was one of the moments when she could see and hear with crystal clarity. There was, however, this thing about her vision: it was like looking through the wrong end of a telescope, everything was clear but reduced and very remote. She could see Coffin, but she had the sense of being miles away. There he was, little and very distinct and here she was, apparently miles away on a cloud and unable to make him hear.

Nor, at this very moment, could she remember why she wanted him to hear, and what. But she felt quite sure she had a good reason and that she would remember it.

Tiny tiny little man, she thought. She leaned out towards the window which she could reach with her hand. Dreamily she thought that the rest of her body felt like lead. Perhaps I'm paralysed, she thought. I feel quite dead.

Quite on its own, her hand fluttered at the window and even gave a rap at the window-pane.

Coffin did not stir. Still he sat at his table and apparently stared straight in front of him.

"Why doesn't he hear?" she asked herself. "Why doesn't anyone hear? Am I a ghost or something?"

But Coffin, sitting at his table, had seen the movement at the window high in the house across the road. He didn't turn his head, but he had seen it all right out of the corner of his eye. He deliberately did not turn his head, because if he did perhaps there would be nothing there and he had no wish to find himself madder than he felt.

Solemnly he studied his Balzac, letting the waters of the *Comédie Humaine*, hardly sparkling and clear, wash over his mind. "Imagine that," he muttered to himself as Cousine Bette's enormities began to appear, "I knew a woman like that, lived off Tower Thames

Road. She lived twenty years with her married daughter and ruined three marriages for her."

Balzac, although not exhilarating, was immensely reassuring. Yes, this is the world, you could say, and I am in it. After only a chapter Coffin was strong enough to swing round and stare suddenly and hard at the house across the street.

"It couldn't be rats," he said aloud. It certainly looked the sort of house that might have rats but he had never known a rat which got up to a window and waved.

Under his bed was his suitcase, all he had now in the way of property. Or rather, all for the moment that he chose to have; in that other world of his that he preferred not to enter, where he was husband, parent and policeman, he owned a number of things. Not much money perhaps, but all sorts of possessions that he had deliberately peeled away from him as if he wanted to throw himself out with his chattels into the dustbin. Now he'd come to live in a street lined with dustbins.

He went on his knees and dragged the suitcase out. There was a heavy tweed overcoat crammed in the top. Goodness knows why he had brought that. It was not a garment he had ever liked and it must now be about ten years old. He threw it out. Underneath were pairs of shoes and socks. They all had holes in. They came out. The next layer was made up of odds and ends of clothes. Even good new clothes don't look their best when rolled up into little balls and these clothes were not new. On the bottom of the case were books and papers. There was also the object he was looking for. He drew it out triumphantly. A battered leather case and inside the case a pair of binoculars. Coffin was not a bird watcher but in his trade there were other things to watch and his glasses were powerful and well kept. That he had them with him was interesting.

He cleaned them with a silk handkerchief—a soft dust seemed to deposit itself over everything in this house and focused them on the window, high in the house opposite.

The girl was still there in the room, sitting alone, since she had nowhere else to go and nothing else to do. The clarity had gone from her vision now, disappearing as quickly as it had come, and although she thought the man across the road must still be sitting there, she could no longer see him. Her head ached and she felt dizzy.

"Oh why am I here in this silly room?" she asked herself, putting a hand to her head. "I never meant to be. It's not my sort of room at all."

What was her sort of room? Suddenly she seemed to see a room with flowered wallpaper and white curtains and a pot of geraniums. *That* was her sort of room.

And my hands ought to be clean, she thought wretchedly. What's the matter with me?

Down below a door banged and she started to tremble.

She had remembered a blow. Something heavy had come savagely down on her head. A blow on her head. She touched it, but all she could feel was a mass of matted hair. Although she wanted to cry she knew she could not and that no tears would ever fall from her again.

The door banged again. Other people could make noises, but she, it seemed, could not.

"Am I a ghost then?" she asked herself desperately. "Is that what I am? How do you know if you're a ghost?" Perhaps you never did, perhaps that was the saddest thing about it.

After the banging of the door came the sound of feet. Someone was coming up the stairs.

She had to ask herself then if ghosts can be truly afraid, or if all they have inside them is the memory of old dead fears.

"There ain't no girl there," said Coffin's landlady. "I tell you there ain't no girl there."

"I saw her. I was watching her."

"How was you watching her?" said his landlady suspiciously.

"With binoculars," said Coffin, and then realised what he had done. She made a hissing noise.

"I don't want anything of that in my house. It's dirty, that is."

"No," began Coffin. "I mean, it isn't that way."

"They always says that. Just scientific interest, they says. Or, *'I'm an artist.'* Are you an artist, then?"

"No."

"Let's have no more of this watching then. Or out you go."

"But the girl."

"There ain't no girl," she said turning away. "How many times have I got to tell you? There ain't no girl that lives opposite. I told you. You're drunk, I expect."

"No." He was indignant. "Of course not."

"You stink of beer." She disappeared up the stairs to her own room. All their conversations were carried on in the hall by the door or on the stairs. It was part of their relationship that she always had her hat and coat on and he was always standing ready to get away from her as soon as possible. This was the first time he had ever sought her out.

He raised his arm to his nose and smelt the beer. It was circumstantial evidence.

"The beer came out of a dustbin," he muttered, but she didn't hear, and if she had what would she have made of it? Something good? No, she would probably have added the dustbin to her mental image of her lodger.

He went back into his room and picked up the binoculars again. Yes, there she was. A still figure, just dimly seen. He could see her face and the upper part of her body, not much else, really. She seemed to be all in white. Remarkable, considering the time of year. But girls these days wore strange garments. Even party dresses looked like shrouds.

"That's a nasty thought," he said slowly, putting down the binoculars.

When he looked again, she seemed to be gone. He looked as far into the room as he could. It seemed to be very sparsely furnished. Through the curtains he could dimly see what must be a bed, a flowered patch of wallpaper, and a door.

The girl must sit near the window in a deep chair. She wasn't there now.

Of course, girls did move about, you had to expect it. She was a girl, probably quite young, and therefore active and mobile.

"If ever I saw a girl who didn't look active and mobile that's the one," said Coffin. He turned back to Balzac. He read Balzac steadily for two hours, then he turned to the window again. It was dark by now and the streetlights were on. He really couldn't see whether she was there or not. But she wouldn't be there in the dark. No one sat in a dark room. There was a light on the ground floor and that was where she must be now, in that lighted room on the ground floor. Tough life for her, he thought.

He fought the desire to look at the house again.

At midnight he jerked his head round and looked across the road. He couldn't stop himself. The streetlights were down, but the light was still on in the room on the bottom floor and the top of the house was still dark.

He fiddled with the binoculars, giving them a thorough polish once more, and raised them to his eyes. Perhaps he wasn't at the right spot at the window. So he lay on the end of the bed and focused them again.

His landlady, who had a little spy-hole of her own in the door, saw him and made a soft little hissing sound of disapproval and pleasure.

He slept well that night. There was something absorbing in the problem of the girl across the road. He wanted to know more about her. Who she was and what she looked like. He'd never had a good view yet. Anyway, she seemed to like him if she waved to him. He didn't dream about her, there was nothing to dream about yet, she was just a girl behind a window and a lot of people said she didn't exist. He slept so well that he slept through the bangings and thumpings that began his landlady's day.

"I'm beginning to get fed up with *him*," she said to her husband, with a nod of her head towards Coffin's room. (She had another lodger, a silent elderly man who sold newspapers on the corner of the street leading to the docks; he had been there for thirty years and weathered many a storm.) "I don't trust him."

"You never does," said her husband. He didn't add: and you don't trust me, because she knew and he knew, their life was founded on it. He drank his hot tea. "No, not never," he said with satisfaction. He was rather proud of his wife's suspicious mind. It was the one thing that stopped their really deadly weekly quarrels ending in a lethal blow. Still, he might kill her one day.

"No," said his wife. Lodgers came and went in their front room. Very few stayed long. They were a weary crowd. Men who had debts and had to lose their own homes, men who had never had a home, men who were running away from their families and men whose families had thrown them out. She never had a woman. "I've never had one as good as Mr Angel." Mr Angel (or perhaps it was Angell or Angle, no one had ever got it quite clear; he hadn't had time to let them see it in writing) had died in the room.

"I never saw Mr Angel," said her husband. "He died before I got a look at him."

"He was the best," said his wife with conviction. Mr Angel, dying, had left behind him a full two weeks rent, paid, a suitcase of clothes and half a bottle of whisky. "But this one—I don't care for him."

"You can always get rid of him."

"Yes." She nodded, "But I feel I'd like to do something *more*."

They both heard her upstairs lodger pad past on his way to sell the morning's papers. After thirty years he knew so much about them both, there was no getting rid of *him*.

"Put the dustbin out when you go," she commanded her husband.

"I put it out yesterday."

"Never mind," said his wife inflexibly. "Put it out again."

Coffin woke as the dustbin crashed down on the pavement. Perhaps he was feeling a little better. At all events he got up briskly and made his bed. He had a wash place behind a screen and here he shaved and dressed. Then he drew the curtains and looked across the road and shook his head at the window. Once, as a policeman, he would have known what to do about the house and the girl, known how to satisfy his curiosity and make it all easy. Nothing was easy now.

He walked out to get some coffee. Because he was late, his usual table by the window was occupied by a large lady with a shopping basket. He had to stand at the counter.

"You haven't got all your books today," said the girl who served him his coffee. "Given up reading?"

He shook his head.

There was a girl in a short red and white skirt with a tight white sweater standing drinking milk at the counter next to him. She looked charming, but he didn't notice that. She was also very interested in him, but of course he didn't notice that either.

She spun round to look out of the window and milk went over his arm. She brushed it off "Oh, sorry. Oh, terribly sorry."

"That's all right." He dried his wrist.

She rubbed at him with a paper tissue, her big blue eyes looking concerned. They could do that well. She had taught them, and she had always been her own best pupil.

"I saw you had a lot of books yesterday. I was interested."

"They were rather dull really, I'm not reading them now." To his surprise, he knew this was true, he wouldn't be reading any more Balzac for the moment.

"I mean I was interested anyone could read so much."

"I haven't." He drank some coffee. But in spite of himself he was interested in her. She had a bright eager face. And after his landlady she smelt good: sweet and fragrant. "Well, perhaps I have. On and off."

"That's better." She smiled over her glass of milk. "I use up so much energy I *have* to drink milk."

"I'm not using up much energy at the moment." He looked down on his coffee. Stimulus there, not much energy perhaps.

"No, I can see that." She studied him. "You look as though you've burnt up plenty in the past, though." She liked that spent tense look he had. It appealed to her imagination.

"What do you do that uses up so much energy?"

She leaned forward, her eyes bright. "Oh, I work in a Welfare Society. We look after people. In fact that's *just* what I do. I help parents look for lost daughters, husbands for wives, that sort of thing."

"You don't look old enough."

"I'm quite trained," she said. He could see now that there were tiny lines by her eyes. She was older than he had thought. She finished her milk. "Well, I must get back to work."

"Any local girls got mislaid round here?" he said slowly, thinking of the house where a girl waved.

"Local? How local?"

"Around here. I don't know." He was vague.

She shouldered her shining black bag. "Not that I know of. I have my troubles but they're not local."

"No." He nodded. It had been an idea.

"There *was* a famous missing-girl story here once. Round the corner in Spicerman Street."

"Go on?" He drank his coffee but kept his eyes on her.

"Yes. A girl quarrelled with her husband, they'd only just been married. Perhaps she'd told him there had been another man or perhaps she said she was unhappy and wanted to run away. Anyway he locked her up and wouldn't let her out. The neighbours didn't know. They'd only just moved in and no one knew anything about them. But she died. He must have hit her on the head or something."

"And what happened to him?"

"He died too. Went out and put himself in the canal. People who were at the wedding said they were a lovely couple and ever so happy." Her voice was composed and cheerful.

"Was the girl imprisoned on the top floor of a house in Spicerman Street? Was it Spicerman Street?"

She shook her head. "I don't know that."

"It was," said Coffin with conviction.

"But that's the tale, rather a sad sweet little story."

"And you call that sweet?" cried Coffin.

"Why, yes!" She was a strange fierce girl, you could, feel the violence in her. "Look, you're a policeman, aren't you? I might need your help myself."

"I'm not working now," he said harshly. "I'm on holiday."

So, he *has* been broken, she thought. Good. I might be able to use him. But I can take my time. "Sorry," she said aloud. But she kept her eyes on him and knew she would approach him again. "See you sometime." It was a meaningless phrase, and Coffin thought she meant nothing by it, but she knew different.

They parted at the street corner. The girl who had served them coffee and milk watched them go.

Coffin walked slowly back to his lodgings. The little encounter had done something for him. Woken him up a little, perhaps.

He turned the corner into Spicerman Street. It didn't exactly feel like coming home, but he was beginning to get the feel of the place.

He looked up at the window.

So there's a ghost up there, he thought. He raised his hand in salute. "Hi there, ghost."

And the ghost waved back.

Chapter 2

"LOOK, SHE WAVED," said Coffin, aloud, as if he wanted to tell everybody. "I saw her." He spoke to the street but no one was there.

He walked across the road and looked up at the window from below. From this angle he could see nothing but dirty curtain. He stepped back, disappointed. But his eye caught sight of something strange in the front garden. Lying there underneath a sagging laurel bush was a woman's nylon stocking. It was neither torn nor dirty, which made it the cleanest thing in sight.

He was holding it in his hand when he went into the house. He was so full of his own thoughts that he did not notice his landlady on the stairs watching him. She made one of her little hissing sounds.

"Oh hello, Mrs Grubb," he said absently, as he looked up and saw her.

"Grout, Grout, not Grubb," she hissed. It was remarkable the dislike she was getting up for her lodger. Perhaps it was because he never seemed to see her. Nor was she a woman to let a good hate go to waste: she wanted something done about it. "Character is what builds a man up," her old schoolteacher used to say, and she thought that if character could build you up she knew how to make it tear you down.

"Drinks and watches girls. He's a menace, I say." She moved down the stairs, accompanied by her own miasma of ammonia and dust. The way she had lived for fifty years had become part of the living flesh by now. She went to her kitchen and started to prepare herself a pot of tea.

Coffin went back to his room, pushed Balzac to the back of the table and sat down to study the stocking. At first glance it looked clean and almost unworn. But when you had a closer look you saw that there was a great torn place across the shin as if someone had kicked it. Well, something or someone had, no doubt about it.

"Wouldn't have liked to be the leg inside that stocking when it copped it," said Coffin aloud, lighting a cigarette. He picked up the stocking again and looked at it. No sign of blood. On an impulse he smelt it. It had been worn.

"Only worn about once," he said, smoking and looking at the back of Balzac. "She ran into something, tore her stocking and threw the stocking away. Nice new pair too. Shame." He thought of what his wife Patsy would say if she laddered a new stocking. He hadn't let himself think about Patsy for days. Now he did, and the thoughts came surging in fast and hot. He covered his face with his hands.

Was this what all the thoughts and preoccupation with the girl over the way were about after all? Were they just cover for thoughts about Patsy? Weren't men deprived of women traditionally supposed to go in for dreams and obsessions? Was he behaving like a soldier in the desert? He considered what his life with Patsy had been these last months and shuddered a little. He did ask himself how much this had contributed to his state now.

He tried to relax and read, but it proved impossible. Against his will he was fidgetty and restless. He read a few pages and scratched himself.

"Confound this," he said, giving his wrist a savage scratch. The itch at once transferred itself to his fingers, to the sensitive area around the nails. All ten spots felt red hot.

He swallowed an aspirin with a drink of water and read on.

But the girl was right there in front of him between him and the book. She was more vivid than Old Goriot this morning. He conceived of her in his mind as a young quiet girl, sitting up there at her window, a latterday Lady of Shalott. He had no doubt that she was somehow looking at a tragedy. Her own or someone else's?

"She's sort of walled up there," he told himself. Then his heart beat faster. No one was walled up these days, not anyone alive. "I'm crazy," he said, not quite liking it aloud, but fearing it might be true. All the same, he couldn't stop thinking about the girl.

The aspirin hadn't really soothed his itch. He attacked his left wrist ferociously. The left seemed the worst, but the right wrist was operating quite a little titillation of its own.

Perhaps it was the scratching but his hands seemed to take up memories of violence of their own. The right one could remember the time he had almost had to strangle a man (had to; *it was him or me, wasn't it?*) the left one could remember the way it had once torn at a man's cheek, and then the right one again could remember all the times he had wanted to hit Patsy, his wife, and hadn't.

Now the thought was right out and very nearly said aloud: he really felt quite violent about Patsy.

"I hate you, Patsy," he said, staring out of the window. "No, that's not quite right. I don't hate you. I don't know what I do feel and that's the hell of it."

At four o'clock he went out. He walked down the road towards the river where at the corner of the street was a small shop which sold cigarettes, newspapers and paperback books promising insight into all types of sin and depravity. Coffin always picked up one to read while he waited to be served, but he hadn't learnt anything yet. There was often a strange divorce between jacket and contents; one day to his surprise he discovered he was reading Tolstoy. He hadn't recognised Anna Karenina under the heading *A Saga of Sex and Sin*.

If he had hoped the walk and the chill air would lull his itch he was wrong. With difficulty he stopped himself scratching as he walked. He held out his arm and looked at his right wrist. There was a thin red weal circling it. The left wrist was the same.

"The stigmata of my itch," he said sardonically, not believing it. At the back of his mind was the idea he had seen a weal like this before.

There was no one in the shop and he was glad; he preferred it that way. He stood there for a minute, drinking in the smell of newspapers and cigarettes. A man appeared behind the counter and stood looking at him. He was a silent man who never spoke before being spoken to, and this was one of the reasons Coffin felt safe going to the shop. The other was that he believed the man was a liar. Each short reluctant sentence he uttered was dubious. Coffin liked this; it made them equal; he wasn't giving away anything and neither was the man.

"Evening paper, please."
"Oh, I haven't got one."
"Under your right hand," said Coffin.
"To spare, I mean. They're all ordered."
Coffin laid his money on the counter. He helped himself to a paper and stood there for a moment reading it. He checked the date thinking that this shop being what it was, this might easily be yesterday's issue, but no, he had today's all right. One day was very much like another to him. But at least he still knew the date and wanted to stay that way.
The man made noiselessly for his chair. He had a little hiding-place behind a display case of books and papers where he lurked, smoking and drinking tea. The fire risk was tremendous; one day it would all go up in smoke. Pale grey lying smoke, Coffin thought.
"Wait a minute," said Coffin to his back. "I want to ask you something."
"Oh yes."
"It's about the house across the road there." He pointed through the window.
"Opposite where you live?"
"You know that?" Coffin was surprised. So there wasn't any anonymity in this shop either.
The man shrugged.
"Who lives in that house then? Who's the girl?"
"No one lives there. Well, hardly anyone. No girl. Young fellow with a widowed mother used to live there. Mother's dead now. Died about ten months ago."
"And the young man?"
"He's still there. If you can call it living. Just somewhere to doss down."

"What sort of a man is he?"

"Quiet. Decent sort. He never says anything to me. I don't know that he ever says anything to anyone. Of course, he was very repressed by his mother."

"Was he?" Goodness knew how much of what was coming across the counter was lies. Nothing sounded true when this man spoke it.

"Oh yes, very repressed. And since she's been gone I don't think he knows what to do with himself." He lowered his voice. "Sometimes he acts as though she's still living there. He's living with her ghost."

"Uncomfortable for him," said Coffin.

"Anyway, you can see for yourself." The man started to move away again. "Just hang on a bit. Read my books like you always do. He comes in here round five-thirty for a paper. Like clockwork. You'll see him." He was going.

"You think I'm going to hang around and wait?"

"Yes." The man looked back at him reflectively. "Yes, I think you might."

Coffin went out and waited on the pavement. He still could read the titles of the magazines and books in the window and he occupied himself with this, shivering a little in the cold wind.

Punctually at five-thirty a man appeared at the corner of the road and walked past Coffin to go into the shop. He was inside a minute, then reappeared carrying a newspaper under his arm. He was everything the shopkeeper had said he was, tidily dressed, round-faced and gentle. Coffin was in his path but he moved round him neatly and deftly, not really looking at him but managing to avoid collision all the same.

"Sorry," said Coffin, but he got no answer.

As well as the newspaper he was carrying a paper bag. A long brown loaf stuck out of it and a bunch of bananas.

"Looks after himself entirely," thought Coffin. "Probably can't cook, just eats things that hardly need it."

Coffin followed silent behind him up the street. He could tell that his noiseless pursuit was noticed. The man's shoulders moved irritably and his feet wove a curving path on the pavement. As if he was drunk. Coffin followed him exactly.

He knows what it is to be frightened, thought Coffin. Now I know that much about him. I know he's had a touch of fear. He quickened his pace. Let's see if I can give him a touch more. He was being deliberately unpleasant.

As they approached the house Coffin looked up at the window. There was nothing to be seen except a stretch of dirty window curtain. Coffin slackened, let the man get ahead, in the garden and to his own front door. He stood on the street watching.

The man turned round from the safety of his own doorstep and gave Coffin a reproachful look. There was no violence in it, just reproach. The wind blew his raincoat open and showed the overalls of someone who worked by his hands. He worked in a factory somewhere, probably the chocolate and biscuit factory just around the corner, and he looked young and poor.

Coffin turned his back and walked across the road. I don't know whether you're living with a ghost or a breathing woman but whichever it is I'm sorry for you.

He knew he had to be sorry for someone. He didn't want to be sorry for himself.

During his absence, Mrs Grout had brooded over her teacups. She had sat about most of the day. In one corner of the room was a big pile of dirty clothes waiting to be washed, in another was a tabby cat with three kittens.

"Here kitty, good kitty," said Mrs Grout, snapping her fingers and making purring noises. She liked cats and made a comfortable squalid home for a great number. They had to be cats that didn't mind milk put in a dirty saucer and food left to go stale, though. Cats that did mind usually packed their bags and left smartly. Many stayed. She was breeding up a race of quiet flea-ridden cats with an eye on the main chance. The pickings were good in the Grout household, provided you looked sharp about it. "Kitty, kitty," she said.

Kitty ignored her and got on with the piece of fish she had filched from the shopping basket so imprudently left on the floor by her box. The kittens were chewing the tail and one of them had already been sick.

Over her tenth cup of tea Mrs Grout decided that she had lost her engagement ring. It was such an obvious decision that she wondered she hadn't thought of it before. Her engagement ring was a thick gold band with two tiny diamonds and a little sapphire. She could no longer get it on her finger. In the first place she had grown too fat and secondly Mr Grout had stood on it one Friday night when he was in a temper. Her left hand had been inside it at the time, but the ring had suffered more than she had and Mr Grout worst of all. The ring was kept in an old purse, together with Mr Grout's life insurance policy and some old French francs which they hoped to make use of some day. Mrs Grout was almost sure that the last time she had looked inside the purse the ring had been gone.

"It's been pinched, that's what," she said with serious satisfaction. "I've been robbed." She got to her feet, slopping tea all over her skirt. "And I don't have to ask myself who's had it. *He's* had it." Nor did she ask herself why Coffin should want her battered ring worth about five pounds at the pawnshop or how he would know where to find it or even how he could have got it when the purse lived between the mattress and her own pillow. It was her deep belief that everything she owned was the object of other people's acquisitiveness, and that if she took her eyes off anything for a minute they would get away with it. "He's had my ring. Well, that's it, out he goes."

She heard the door open and was out of her kitchen and along the hall before her lodger could even get the door closed.

"Here," she said, "I'll have you up for taking my ring."

"What ring?" cried Coffin.

"I ought to have known the sort you were. Drinking. Looking at girls. You've gone too far, taking my ring. I can make trouble for you." She said it with satisfaction. It wasn't only that she wanted him out, she wanted him in trouble too.

"I haven't touched your ring." It sounded weak even as he said it. He'd heard other men make that sort of remark and had never believed them. Now he knew how it felt. He wasn't surprised to hear her laugh. He threw open the door of his room. "Here, take a look." Another weak gesture, men on the defensive always said something similar.

"No." She was scornful. "You wouldn't let me look if you knew I'd find it."

"That seems it, then," said Coffin sourly.

"Don't you believe it," She pushed him aside and swaggered into the middle of the room. "You ought to be in the hands of the police." She spoke the words with pleasure. It interested her to think of hands roughly attacking this stranger she hated.

Coffin was bewildered. He didn't know he was hated; he was learning it, though.

"Keep your hands off me. You touch me again and I'll have the whole street in on you."

"I didn't touch you. I was just walking past." But he had touched her, only a brush, just enough to tangle up the truth.

"They'll do to you what they did to that black boy that come walking down here. He fell in the gutter."

"I won't fall in the gutter."

"You can get out."

"I'm collecting my things."

She put out her hand. "You can leave them. In place of the ring."

"But you said..." She had him coming and going.

"I've changed my mind."

There was a slight pause. Outside in the street doors

were banging behind men coming home from their work. There were some children on roller skates.

"Don't stand there looking at me. Just go."

Without answering her he picked up his case and threw his few possessions into it. He tucked the volumes of Balzac under his arm. She didn't try to stop him.

At the front door he turned: "You've got my rent, you can keep that."

Carrying his case and clutching his books, Coffin walked out into Spicerman Street and away.

His landlady stumped upstairs to her own quarters. She noticed that the cat had stolen the fish, but she was too triumphant with her victory to bother. She gave the basket a kick, moving her ankle away quickly to avoid the paw that shot out, and went over to the bed to look in her purse of valuables.

The insurance policy was there, nicely folded over, and there were the worthless French francs. She knew they were worthless but she couldn't bring herself to admit it.

Tucked away in the corner of the purse was the ring.

"Funny," she said cheerfully. "It was there all the time." She smiled. Then an intent look came over her face and she made for the door again. "I'll just have a look round his room."

She went into what had been Coffin's room. He hadn't lived in it long but even to her it was still more his room than her own. The window was wedged open with a piece of paper, blowing out the stale air that seemed to hang over the rest of the house. The furniture was free of dust if not polished and the bed was neatly made. In spite of his hurry to go Coffin hadn't left anything behind. Nothing personal. There was a rolled up newspaper and an empty cigarette packet. She pulled open a drawer but it was empty and looked as though it had always been empty except for a colony of mice that might have lived in it once. Now even they had gone. All the drawers were empty. The cupboard was bare too.

"What, no bottles?" she said. "He drinks, though. I smelt it."

Silently she nipped up the stairs to the top floor where her other lodger lived. *He* had plenty of bottles, a whole shelf full of empties. Some were broken as if he had thrown them into position. Probably he had. There were often crashes and bangs from the top floor but no one ever dared go up while the top floor tenant wrestled with the private devils which pursued him. They were powerful devils, and often made him moan.

Mrs Grout took an armful of bottles, sidled down the stairs and popped them into what had been Coffin's cupboard.

"Might as well give him a few bottles," she said. "Who's going to believe me when I say he drinks if there ain't any bottles?"

No one was going to believe her because no one was going to know. She was building up this picture entirely for herself. To add another convincing detail she rolled a bottle under the bed.

There she saw a stocking. Just one woman's stocking of pale nylon.

She made her little hissing sound of disapproval and joy.

"A woman's stocking," she said; there was satisfaction in her voice. She sat back on her heels. "I knew the sort he was. I was right. He's one of those queer ones."

From her position on the floor she could see straight across and up to the windows in the top of the house opposite. The windows were all dark.

She moved her hand across her eyes as if to clear them. Then she got to her feet and scuttled out of the room, closing the door behind her.

"Could start imagining things if you sat there staring," she told herself. "You could really imagine you saw things."

In the girl's mind, wherever it was now situated (and she herself was beginning to fear it was no living body but suspended somewhere in limbo) a memory was forming, distinct and unmistakable.

She remembered a physical attack. The details were coming through, savage and clear. She remembered a pain in her head, she remembered hands that grabbed her.

What she couldn't get clear was whether she was awake or asleep?

Or dead.

"Am I a dead girl or a live one?" she asked. It wasn't really a question worth asking, but somehow she felt that even in putting it she was doing herself a service. "And if I'm a live one, why doesn't anyone come when I call? Or answer when I wave?"

At this period rational ideas and memories came and went, floating into her mind like birds and floating out again.

This moment she knew she had been the victim of an attack. She had been somebody's victim.

She feared another attack. She feared attack and this time a sexual attack. She knew it was coming. It must be.

"Wasn't I going to be married?" she asked herself. "Or did I refuse to be married?"

She struggled to get attention. She tried very hard to wave.

Any outsider watching the room from the street below, not Mrs Grout, and not Coffin who was gone, would certainly have said there was a movement of some sort within the room.

So now Coffin knew what it felt like to be turned out into the streets and to be frightened of a lying screaming woman. It was a new kind of fear for him, not the sharp straightforward physical sort he had felt when going into a bad fight with the odds against him and the other man with a knuckleduster, and not the sort he had felt as the bullet scorched through his body. They, in their way, were the sort of fear a man could be expected to bear. Now he had got to know a new dirty crawling sort of fear.

"If I'd had just a little more luck in my life I might never have known I had that in me," he said, stirring his cup of pale coffee. Or perhaps it wasn't luck. If you knew the worst about yourself you hadn't any farther to go, had you? What was the worst about himself? "That's the question, boy," he muttered.

The girl sitting opposite him on the other side of the little table smiled. She had a pretty smile. She had so arranged her lipstick that even when she stopped smiling her lips had a curve to them. Her eyes had an upward tilt as well, like a cat's, but that too was make-up. It was possible that underneath it all she had round cold eyes and thin lips.

"Every evening I come here," she said. "It's the first evening you've been here. I thought you were only a mornings bird."

"I'm not a bird at all." He was sour. "Never have been, never could be. Never had wings, never had a song."

"You certainly haven't right now." She pressed her lips sweetly together. "What crippled you?"

"Running," he said. "Running too hard."

"You've stopped now." She had a good look at his face. Perhaps he had stopped running forward forever.

Coffin's wrists were still worrying him. He put his hands in his lap; he didn't want her to see the red weal.

"Something wrong?" She missed nothing.

"No."

"You could help me." She smiled at him.

"No help."

"I'd pay you."

"I don't want money."

"You look as though you could do with some all the same," she said, appraising him. "You don't have to be honest or reliable or trustworthy or anything like that."

"Now I know."

"No need to be bitter. You should see yourself. But I will say this, you still look as if you could see through a brick wall." She was staring at him hopefully. "Now you just listen: it'll interest you."

"Nothing is that interesting."

"Yes." She studied his face. "Well, I can see you might feel like that. But this is it: you know now what my work is; well, you know part of it. Trying to join families together again. I don't do the detective work. I'm just an administrator. No," she hesitated, she did truly think she was much more than an administrator. "More like a sort of doctor. My name is Alberta McCree."

"Oh, you're important, I can see," said Coffin.

"I do good work. Sometimes I help people get track of each other, but not often, other people do that. My job starts when we find the one that's lost. But that's when my real troubles start."

"I can imagine."

"We had a mother living in Wolverhampton. Her daughter had left home. We found her. It wasn't difficult, but it took time."

"How much time?"

"Say about nine months. We had the girl's name, description and photograph. We knew the sort of work she could do, she was a good typist, and that was how we found her. The mother's name was Rigby, Mrs Elizabeth Rigby, she's a widow, and she had asked us to help with her daughter Jess Rigby."

"And you found her."

For the first time she hesitated. "We found a girl called Jess Rigby who works as a typist and who lives in a room on her own and has been there less than six months and more than three. Mrs Rigby hasn't seen her yet but she says she knows it's her girl. Jess says she isn't. She says she's going to produce perfectly good parents of her own and will we leave her alone."

"She will, then, and that will be it."

"No. I don't think so somehow."

"Does she look like the photograph Mrs Rigby gave you."

"No. Not very. Not unlike either."

"But Mrs Rigby hasn't seen her yet, has she? She can't really tell."

"We showed her a snapshot of the girl. Taken on the roof of where she works. She chose the right girl at once out of a group of others."

"It's easy, you just get the two together, then something will give."

"Mrs Rigby's an invalid. Been in and out of hospital for years."

"Oh." Coffin was thinking: a helpless widow wouldn't be likely to be keeping her house going. For that you need friends, husbands, love. Money too. There probably wouldn't be much money in the Rigby family. "Doesn't sound as if the girl had much of a home to leave. Where did she live?"

"With an aunt. She's dead now. There was some sort of a family life."

"You think the girl is lying, don't you?"

"I think Mrs Rigby is telling the truth," she said, giving him a radiant smile. "Let's put it that way. As she sees it."

"She's certainly giving everyone a lot of trouble."

"She has no luck."

"Whichever way you look at it," said Coffin sourly, "she's lost a daughter."

His companion smiled. A beautiful smile that began small, then flowered and finally closed.

She's up to something, thought Coffin. I wonder what it is? I may never know. Aloud, he said: "What is it you want me to do?"

"You mean you're going to help?" She leaned forward eagerly.

"No, I didn't say that. I just want to establish your intentions."

"You're a poor broken-down copper and I'm offering you a job," she said softly.

"You won't get me."

"I will. I might." She smiled again and stood up. "We'll keep in touch. I'll find you."

"I'm going away."

"I've got my methods..." She was gathering her parcels together. Obviously she had been shopping before she came here. She had bread, lettuce, tucked under her arm. Blood from a thick piece of meat seeped through the paper. She was leaving. "I should see a hospital about that itch on your wrist," she said, and walked towards the door.

Alberta went home, got on with preparing her supper, confident she had made a start on her plans with Coffin. She didn't know how she would find him if he went away, but she felt confident she could do it. She was a girl who always managed to do what she wanted.

Afterwards she sat down to write letters. She kept up a great correspondence with friends from school and college, she loved to get letters and keep friends, but inside she was quite lonely.

"I think I am capable of love," she said aloud, "but I may not be capable of affection." She remembered saying something like this once to her mother (before her mother died) and her mother had looked puzzled and asked, "But is there much difference?" (Well, for her mother there wasn't, of course.) Alberta had said there was a difference between them like a great hungry mouth. "All the better to eat you with, my dear," she had pointed out, laughing.

She needed Coffin in her coffer with Jess Rigby. She couldn't let him into any secrets, but she could let him into that one. She got out her notes and studied once again the case of this girl. She smoked two cigarettes while she considered it.

She had to have aid for her side. It wasn't so much the mother, who was weak and ailing (although very articulate), but the phalanx of help assembled behind her, all the nurses and doctors and matrons and social workers, who could be counted upon to give her strength and support. Mrs Rigby very possibly had right on her side, too and this was going to support her. Who was going to help the wrong? Coffin was elected.

In the crystal ball the old woman, who had seen nothing for days, suddenly saw the girl in the attic move and stir as if with life.

It was a life of a sort. Life without much of a future. The girl's memory had returned.

"I am a prisoner," she stated. "I did not come here, I was brought. I was captured. I am now a captive."

She swivelled her head round. She knew now she was tied up and locked in this room. At some time, probably when she was captured; this she did not remember. Subsequently, she had been drugged.

"No. Not captured," she said, suddenly and brilliantly. "I came here to tea. To tea. No, not tea. A drink. I was asked round here for a drink." She put her hand to her head. "Why, he kept me," she exclaimed in horror. "I remember now, he said: you cannot go away, I claim you as my bride." She began to sob. She was terrified and afraid of being either a woman or a ghost. "He says he loves me, but he doesn't love anyone. He's mad." Now she was seeing it clear.

In anybody's crystal ball her future looked hopeless.

Coffin thought he wasn't watched, but there were eyes on him. Eyes that did not use a crystal ball.

"He's moved away from Spicerman Street," said his immediate superior, Chief Superintendent Styles, to Coffin's wife, Patsy. "We've lost him for the moment, but don't worry."

"He doesn't answer my letters," she said. "Just doesn't answer."

"He may not be getting them."

"I don't like it," said Patsy. "He's getting worse, not better. You told me to leave him alone, that it would help. Has it?"

"He's had a bad time. Concussion. Illness ... Leave him be."

Patsy said nothing.

"He was torn up by that case last year, wasn't he? The one where the young girl was attacked and killed. I thought that left a mark on him. Some cases do, you know, you have to accept it. Policemen are only human. And she was terribly injured."

"Yes." She was quiet. "He did mind about that. It was strange."

"No, not strange." He was quiet too and thought she was a woman who had imagination only for herself or her child. Plenty like that. "Strain shows itself in funny ways. He might do something we don't expect."

"He's doing that," said Patsy, turning away. "He's doing that all the time."

"I expect there are limits you have set for his behaviour though," explained the Chief Superintendent carefully. "Limits you have set whether you know it or not. He might go beyond those limits, that's what I'm telling you."

It was a warning.

A man was looking for Coffin; he had no name. That is, he liked to think he had no name. He had been perfectly adequately christened Edward Arnold Jones, but he had deliberately lost his name early on in his career because he believed it was not his own. He was a changeling and had had very distinguished parents, probably of royal blood. Why he had been abandoned he didn't know, but it in no way detracted from his position. For someone like him there were special privileges. Women, for instance. He could do what he liked about women and no one could interfere. This was known as *Droit de seigneur*. (He had read the phrase somewhere and found it at once applicable to him.) If this sometimes involved violence and came very near to rape, he still did not hesitate. As a result of choosing his victims carefully there had never yet been a complaint to the police.

Coffin had never investigated him, never even met him, but nevertheless in the course of his duties he had several times got in the other's way. Paradoxically the nameless man lived in Coffin's district and knew plenty of detail about the policeman. He had made it his business to learn because he was building up a resentment. He was beginning to have a really dangerous feeling about him. He started to watch Coffin's house.

Chapter 3

COFFIN SLEPT THAT NIGHT in a lodging house where you could get a bed for three shillings. He was late getting there, very late, the last man in. The bed was very clean and very hard and only a thin panel of painted wood separated him from the sleeper next door. Nothing separated him from the sound of his snoring. The man next door was drunk. He was always drunk. Over everything was the smell of strong carbolic, still the basic disinfectant, science can produce no cheaper, and damp. The lodging house was run by the same charitable foundation for which Alberta worked. Coffin did not know this. Perhaps he would not have cared. The law by which their lives were to be kept in touch was already operating.

He passed a restless night, what with his wrists and his dreams. Not to mention the tenant on the right-hand side. His neighbour was having a ball. Every so often he gave a loud happy laugh. You could hear he was trying to keep it under, but it was no good, the laugh would burst out.

Then he sang the chorus of a song. The song was unrecognisable but you could tell it was the chorus because of the way he sang it. He was terribly happy there inside his little cubicle.

On Coffin's other side there was complete silence. At first there had been snoring, now silence. Coffin thought that the man might be dead. It would be morning before anyone looked to see. "Well, it won't be me," he said to himself "I won't be the one that looks." He closed his eyes. Next door the ball closed down.

In the street outside he could hear a street-cleaning van moving slowly along, pouring water as it went. He was near a street market here. Fruit, vegetables and fish were sold on open stalls, just as they had been for centuries. Once flaming gas jets had lit and warmed the stalls, now each had its little circle of electric lights. Very soon, although it was still dark, he could hear voices and movements. The new day was beginning out there in the street market. He had shopped there himself as a boy and had once had a job as an errand boy to a fruit seller. Prior, the old boy had been called. The job had ended on Christmas Eve when Coffin fell off his bike carrying a load of Christmas trees and broke his arm. He could feel the pain of that break now and the smell of the green trees as they fell about him and smell the beer on old Prior's breath as he had peered anxiously down at him. He went to hospital, ate his Christmas dinner there and never got his wages. He suddenly felt very very angry about those wages which he ought to have had. After thirty years they burned a hot angry hole in his mind. "Mean old devil," he muttered. "That was Prior all over. Lived to be ninety and went up with a bomb in 1940."

The place where Coffin was lying was made up of one great room subdivided into little cubicles. Obviously it hadn't been built for people to sleep in. What had it been built for, then? "A mortuary," said Coffin sleepily. A sort of mausoleum. No, now he remembered, it had been a little factory and had made clothes for children. He fell asleep.

The warden in charge came down the centre aisle, checking quietly to see if everything was in order. He knew Coffin by sight, having seen him once in court, and had been mildly puzzled by his appearance here tonight. But he supposed he was on some sort of work, following a wanted man perhaps. Without very much curiosity he wondered which of his other charges was the suspect. Dull lot in tonight. Could hardly raise a boo to a goose among them. He could remember the days...

He opened the window at the end of the room and a smell of fruit and vegetables and soft rain floated in. There was some sort of row going on in the market. Or if not a row. then voices were raised and excited. He thought nothing of it. There were rows and raised voices almost every night in the market.

An ambulance hurried down the main road beyond the market, he could see the distant flashes of its warning light. "An accident," he thought placidly. He was a calm man. He was, however, very strong, and this, together with his calmness, stood him in very good stead with his intemperate charges.

On his way out of the room he paused to look in on Coffin, thinking that if he was still awake they might perhaps have a chat. About business, of course.

But Coffin was sound asleep, hands on the sheet in front of him. The warden looked down on him in a friendly way. He could see the inflamed wrists.

"Nasty," he said, turning to go, "Wonder how he picked that up?" He scratched his own arm. There were plenty of reasons for scratching in this place, a few hopped in every evening.

Coffin woke up after some hours sleep, washed (the water was hot, the soap coarse), drank some hot, sweet tea and departed. The rain had stopped and it was a warm easy morning.

"No, I won't be back," he said to the man who kept the records.

"Looking for work?"

"No." He hardly bothered to answer. "Not work."

"Well, you should get those wrists looked at."

Coffin walked away.

"For the sake of other people," called the man after him.

"I'm just going to," said Coffin over his shoulder.

As a figure in a crystal ball he was a failure; you didn't have to be a seer to follow him. He was moving around, not doing anything exciting, leaving a trail a mile wide.

Predictably Coffin walked two hundred yards, crossed a busy main road and went into the Canute Hospital. It is very easy to be mindless and not know what you are walking into when you are a figure in a crystal ball. Coffin was mindless. Sometimes a thought of Alberta yesterday crossed his mind but nothing went very deep. Yes, it was odd about the girl Jess Rigby and her mother, but the answer was easy: she was crazy. Still it made an interesting picture; the mother anxious to identify a girl as her daughter and the girl who had the right name and very nearly the right face and who was refusing to be the daughter. Perhaps she had a double. A *Doppelgänger* was always useful. Every refugee should be provided with one.

Although it was early in the morning, the Outpatients' Clinic at the Canute was already crowded with casualties from the night before. One man was holding a pad to his eye and there was blood on it. Another was propping his leg up on the bench as if it hurt him. A third was already installed on a trolley and waiting for a nurse to wheel him away.

"Gotta get me X-ray," he said; he knew the ropes. "But I'm in a state of shock. I think. I ought to be treated for shock first. I'm so cold." The nurse wheeled him away without speaking, without even looking at him. He disappeared through a door and no one saw him again. Even before Coffin left the hospital a disconcerting rumour came back that he was dead. But the hospital was like that; rumours were thrown about it like balls. They were never happy rumours.

Coffin sat very still and waited for his turn. It was going to be one of those sultry autumn days that come to the city sometimes. Already he was sweating. The man on the trolley had been cold—he was hot.

The man with the pad on his eye went over to get a drink.

A policeman appeared at the end of the room and looked down the room. He then walked slowly through as if he was looking for someone. Coffin joined the man with the eye injury at the water fountain and drank some water until the policeman was safely past. It wasn't much of a way of hiding. Stupid, really. He was beginning, without quite knowing why, to feel hunted.

The side window by the water fountain had a view straight down the main road. If he looked at the roofs he imagined himself a crow who could see Spicerman Street. He threw the paper cup into the bin and walked away. Spicerman Street had been a mistake.

There was a girl in Spicerman Street and whether she was a woman or a ghost she had already brought him trouble.

"I was wrong to go away from there without trying to speak to her," he said to himself "I could have got in through a window easily, gone up the stairs and had it all out with her. Was she waving or wasn't she waving?"

It wasn't difficult to imagine the room, which for some reason he saw as empty, except for a narrow bed by the window. No chair.

"So that's why sometimes you could see her and sometimes you couldn't," he decided. "She was lying down or sitting up, according to how she felt." He gave a sceptical look. "Feeling? What am I talking about? She didn't feel anything, she was just a little automaton. Probably didn't really exist."

All those houses in Spicerman Street were the same. He supposed there was a narrow staircase lit only by one narrow window and not carpeted beyond the first flight. But why was he thinking of carpet? Didn't this house have a thin strip of linoleum running all the way up? You could fall on those stairs and slide from top to bottom.

He felt as if he had fallen on them. On the top floor was one door behind which the girl sat waiting.

"Yes, she is there," he affirmed. "There's someone up in that room. But she's no business of mine. I'll give old Ma Grubb that much." (He could never get her name right, but it was too late to bother now.) "She was right there. I shouldn't have been looking."

What was there about the girl? It couldn't be

anything personal as he could hardly see her. Probably she had a better view of him though. But that was hardly an introduction. She wasn't having much of a life up there, was she? If she was having one at all. And on that point, there seemed two points of view.

"I don't believe in ghosts," said Coffin. "I believe in dead girls or live ones."

But there was something on his mind about the girl in Spicerman Street. He associated her with violence. Perhaps because he already knew that a woman had died violently in that house. This was what happened to people who got to know too much about violence as he had: they began to think excessively about it. If it hadn't happened to him then it would have shown itself in his son, or his wife. Somehow it had to come out. He was glad it was coming out through him. He was now ready to think absolutely about violence and what it meant to him. He tried to do this.

But at the moment it meant the girl in Spicerman Street.

"She might just be a stand-in for Patsy," he said. "I recognise that, I have to."

"I'm sorry you've had such a long wait," said the nurse. "We're ready now."

Coffin muttered something about not minding and held out his wrists.

"Oh yes, scabies," said the doctor briskly. "Nasty little brutes, but you won't die of it."

"How'd I get it?"

"You tell me."

"Somewhere dirty." He was detached. Not interested. Scabies, although unpleasing, was not a notifiable disease. You did not report it and the World Health Organisation was not concerned.

"You'll be able to think."

"Yes, I will." Spicerman Street. Mrs Grout. The house where only the clean in mind and body were welcome.

"I'll give you something to paint on it." The doctor nodded to the nurse. He himself was keeping well away. "Hello, you've hurt yourself?"

"Hurt myself? No."

Coffin looked down at the cuff of his coat.

"Not my blood."

"Your wrist, though."

"My wrist. Not my blood."

On the cuff of his coat was a thick oval stain of blood.

Outside the hospital again, he started to walk. There was no special aim or direction for his walk. You could hardly call it a stroll, yet he didn't seem to be going anywhere either. He might have been filling in time, only what he was waiting for wasn't clear.

He had the impression of having slept even worse than he had, and what was more, of having dreamed. The dream was gone, leaving behind only the feeling that it had been a bloody murderous dream.

He came to a stop at one point and smoked a cigarette on a street bench. The sun shone, it was a lovely day.

The vacuum in time was soon to be filled.

The first editions of the evening papers came on the street around midday and he bought one from a boy with a barrow.

BODY FOUND IN SOUTH LONDON STREET, he read. GIRL FOUND STRANGLED.

The body, beaten as well as strangled and only lightly clothed, had been found under a railway arch. The name of the street wasn't given, but there was a photograph and he knew it at once for Spicerman Street. Besides, where else could it be?

This was what he had been waiting for.

Meanwhile Mrs Grout was busy talking to the police. She could describe her tenant and give full voice to her dark suspicions. She didn't seem to know her lodger's name. (But he had never known hers.) He had paid in advance and she didn't care what he was called. No doubt he had told her, but she had forgotten.

"Anyway I told him to go. He wasn't a right sort, see. He kept on and on about the girl he could see in the window. I told him there wasn't one."

"Where was this girl?"

"And he killed her," said Mrs Grout perversely. "Killed her with a stocking like them I found and went away and left his beer bottles." She kicked at the bottles, which rolled triumphantly round the room.

"Where was this girl?"

"It's a house across the road. One chap on his own. He's out at work all day. You can see him at five-thirty."

"Did you see the girl?"

Mrs Grout shook her head.

Upstairs her other tenant lay on his bed and moaned loudly as his devils attacked him. They had been on the warpath all day. His devils were frightened of violent death when it came too close to home.

Within a very few hours of his first visit Coffin's

superior officer called on Patsy again.

"He's been seen at a hospital. Went for treatment."

"He's ill again?"

"No. Nothing to do with the accident. Quite different. Picked up scabies."

"What's he been doing?" She was near tears. They were real tears but you always had to remember she was an actress. Actresses do cry real tears.

"We don't quite know that." The truth can be, and often is, an evasion.

"Do you know where he is now?"

"No. He's gone again."

"I want to see him."

He was silent, wondering exactly how to put it. "Have you ever thought he might attack you?"

"No." She was not acting. "No."

He leaned forward and lowered his voice. "I think we have to take into account that he might attack you."

Chapter 4

AS IT HAPPENED, the evidence of the crystal ball was delivered for judgement to the same policeman who had to consider the killing of the girl found dead in Spicerman Street, Chief Superintendent Styles. If you wonder why the evidence of the crystal ball got so high in the police hierarchy the answer lay in the unsteadily crowned head that had looked into the crystal ball. The identity of the seer was known to the police.

Styles was a level-headed man who didn't like crystal balls and didn't like lies either. Leaving detail, it may be said that they had met in the past and that the lady with the crystal ball had left no doubt in the policeman's mind that she knew how to tell lies.

Now he had a murder fulfilling her prediction. Here was a girl, dressed in a white slip and nothing else. She had been murdered, perhaps she had been kept somewhere before being murdered.

To do him justice, he did remember the prediction. But only to dismiss it.

"The only murder she knows anything about is the one she did herself," he said. "Who poisoned the old biddy that lived with her?"

But this was a problem on which proof had long been wanting (although speculation had not), so he turned to the one on which he had hoped to have proof. He was prepared to look for it patiently and carefully but he certainly expected to find it.

He wanted to know who had killed this girl, how, and why.

Mrs Grout thought she knew and she was continually offering her proof to anyone, neighbour, policeman, newspaperman, who would listen.

"It was him that did it, that man who stayed here. I knew he was dangerous." She spent the whole day with her hat and coat on, standing on the street corner giving her version to all. "He might have killed *me* if he'd stayed in the house. But something warned me."

Her top-floor lodger slunk past on his way home. He could hear what she was saying. He gave her a grimace and a nod. Business had been good today and he was more than average drunk, but unlike his landlady he was not of an excitable disposition. He was not one to be up today and down tomorrow; he maintained a steady low.

Halfway through the morning she had deserted Spicerman Street (which was getting bored with her anyway) and padded round the corner to the sweet factory.

"Want to see John Kedge," she had said to the man at the gate. "Can you get him for me?"

"Can't do that, Mrs."

"It's important. You can do it."

"It's not allowed." But the man knew who she was and hesitated.

"Oh, go on."

"Wait here."

In a few minutes John Kedge appeared, blinking and looking surprised.

Mrs Grout stared at him with interest and satisfaction. "Here, I've come to tell you something. After you came to work this morning they found a

dead girl underneath the arch—you know where."
He looked as if he had not understood.
"The police will be looking for you. Clear off. That's what I'm telling you! Don't go home."
He still did not answer.
"Make a run for it."
John Kedge's face was thin and tense.
"Why have you come?" he asked in a thick voice.
"I told you."
"No. That's not why you've come."
"Do you still keep a key by your front doorstep, a spare key to get in with?"
"It was there last time I looked," he said.
"Then someone could have got in your house, couldn't they? And had a look round? And found whatever you'd got there? If you had anything."
"Someone like you?"
"No. Not me. What about the man who was in my house? I bet you know what he looked like. You ought to look out for him. He might be the one that killed the girl. The police are going to say it's either you or him. Why don't you find him before they do?"
She watched him turn and walk away from her. He started to walk faster and faster so that as he got to the door of the factory he was almost running.
"Well, you didn't get much change out of that, did you?" said the gate-man, who had of course been listening.
"You shut your trap," said Mrs Grout. "Didn't I help you out with your Margie?" She had many little backstreet roles and the capacity in which she had helped Margie was one of them.

"Oh, that was you?" said the man uncertainly. "I didn't know that was you."

"Now you know," said Mrs Grout and minced off.

The place under the railway arch where the girl had been found had been screened off from the public. Police technicians were still at work there. This arch had been built a hundred years ago when the railways first straddled London. Outside it was dirty yellow brick and inside a lining of grubby broken white tiles. Still, it had survived two great wars and plenty of bombs and looked capable of going on as long as a Roman aqueduct. There was a deep recess on either side, made necessary perhaps by some structural reason, and it was in this, on the south side of the arch, that the girl had been found, her body hidden beneath sacking and old paper. She could have been there for days, but in fact she had only been there a few hours before being discovered by a man with his dog.

All day policemen had been up and down Spicerman Street and neighbouring Avon Street and Shakespeare Road asking questions. So far they could discover nothing to identify the girl. She didn't live locally.

Spicerman Street was checked over. The Walshes at No. 3, the Bells at No. 5, the Kittos, Farmers and Oppes at No. 7, and so on down the street had all been interviewed. The Swallows and the Doves at No. 2, the Frasers at No. 4, and the Sharretts at No. 6 had all arrived home from work, heard the news if they didn't know it already, and seen a policeman. No finger-prints had been taken and not many questions asked, it was just a first quick going-over.

The police were looking for anything that stood out.

The man in No. 14, which was the house where John Coffin thought he had seen a girl, was not at home. His neighbour at No. 12 said he was called John Kedge and worked at the sweet factory round the corner. "Home at five-thirty," he said. It was the one fact all of Spicerman Street knew about him: that he always came home at five-thirty.

But John Kedge did not come home at five-thirty, or six-thirty. By seven-thirty he was still not at home. An inquiry at the sweet factory produced the news that he had come in to work as usual but had left at the dinner break and not come back. For reasons of his own (and Margie's) the gate-man did not tell of Mrs Grout's visit.

At eight-thirty the police quietly let themselves into No. 14 through a downstairs window.

Mrs Grout stood on the kerb watching them. So did most of Spicerman Street.

No. 14 Spicerman Street was more quietly dirty than any house in the street. Mrs Grout's house was dirty but at least it was a lived in dirt; in No. 14 the dirt lay accumulated and was stepped over, as if it was a natural growth that must not be disturbed. A good deal of it, like the mould and fungi under the stairs, was of natural growth. The pile of newspapers and the empty tins and the old furniture were not. The stairs were relatively clean, as if a careful right of way had been preserved.

One room on the top floor contained a good bed with a bed-table piled with books. There was a carpet on the floor and a big easy chair drawn up by a gas-fire. It was just as grubby and untidy as everywhere else but someone had tried to be comfortable in it. The really striking thing about it, though, was that the wall near the chair was covered with pictures of girls cut from newspapers and magazines. Nearest to the chair a group of a dozen pictures had been formed into a circle.

"Look. All one girl," said Styles.

They were all pictures of the same girl wearing a bathing-suit or full skirted evening dress and looking fair and gentle and rather frightened.

Miss Ann Paton, Beauty Queen.

Winner of Beauty Contest in Rococo Ballroom. Miss Lollipop. London girl beauty winner in Sugar Industry.

Ann Paton, aged 19: 34, 24, 34. Orphan and living alone. Shall travel with prize money, she says. And, *Ann Paton, Pretty fair-haired golden-eyed winner of Beauty Contest for girls working in the sweet trade said yesterday she would spend her prize money 'travelling' and she hoped to go in for the Miss World Contest later in the year. "Yes, I've had hundreds of letters and invitations and a proposal of marriage since I won, but I don't mean to get married just yet," she laughed.*

"It's her all right," said Styles.

"Poor Miss Lollipop," said someone else.

"You think this man here's the killer?" asked a third.

"I shall think so unless Mr Kedge returns with a good explanation," said Styles.

He trudged upstairs. Shiny linoleum covered the bare boards. In the top floor front room he stood looking around. There was a bed, but not much else in the room. It was pretty dirty.

"A girl's been here." He picked up a golden hair from the bed. "How long would you say?"

"Difficult to answer. Not long, say two or three days. Three or four."

"Bad thing for John Coffin."

"What d'ye say?"

"Nothing." Styles went to the window and looked down at Mrs Grout's front room. "It's been bad for him all round," he said under his breath.

"Here's a woman's handbag," called his colleague. "Under the pillow."

Styles watched him as he opened it. The bag was of dark blue calf, a good bag, perhaps one of Miss Lollipop's prizes. Inside was a lipstick, a pocket diary with a pencil, a little metal box full of powder, and a purse with two pound notes and some coins.

"Poor silly girl," said Styles. "Coming here. Putting your head in the lion's den."

"How was she to know he wouldn't let her walk out again."

"You think that was it?"

"Look at the door." It had a thick new bolt on the outside. There was no key.

Styles opened the diary. It opened easily at the centre pages. On these pages someone had written in pencil. *I will not marry him, I cannot marry him* it said. *He says he will keep me here...*

Underneath, in large block letters, it said NO MARRY NO MARRY NO MARRY.

"We can't pack it up, and put it away yet," said Styles. "We've got to find this man John Kedge. If he's still alive. He could be dead. But I get a picture, don't you?

He's a crazy boy and picks on this unlucky girl because she wins a prize for her pretty face. There'll be a reason, plenty probably, when we go into it all..."

He stood firmly on the floor of this room in which a girl had been imprisoned.

"Go through the records. Find out if we have anything on Kedge. Check on the house. I seem to remember this street. Go back about ten to fifteen years."

He walked down the stairs and into Spicerman Street. In its history it had experienced many forms of violent death. This was its second murder. Both were connected with the same house. It was a house of nasty character, no doubt about it.

Later that day Styles went round to see Patsy Coffin again. She greeted him warily.

"He's in the clear," he said. But he still sounded worried. "I haven't got it straight what happened in that house yet. I don't know where your man comes into it. If he does. But we'll have to find him. He must be in a bad way. Let me know if he gets in touch with you."

Patsy was silent.

"Will you?"

"Yes."

"Have you any idea where he might have gone?"

"No. None."

"I'd like to find him. For his own sake."

"Yes."

"You don't sound keen."

"I want him to come home. Not be fetched home.

Something wrong in that? He ought to be free. At least I feel that."

You're learning, said Styles, to himself.

"There's one person he could go to and no questions asked," said Patsy.

"The Princess?"

"Oh, you know that too? You know her? The old one."

Styles was silent. "Queer set-up there," he said. "You know she always claims extra-territorial rights in that house. Like an embassy. Says she is really a *de facto* head of state. It's not accepted, of course. But she gets away with a lot there. Gets away with murder. I think she *has* got away with murder."

"It's a sort of sanctuary there," said Patsy.

"Certainly that old woman she had living with her, she called her a lady-in-waiting..."

"She *was* a lady-in-waiting once," put in Patsy.

"Well, she died. She was poisoned. Most people believe the old Princess Regina did it. God knows why. Probably meting out some form of justice. No doubt she thinks she's a source of law and justice as well as being a sovereign state. A mini-sovereign state."

"He might go there. They were friends." Patsy was silent. She knew well enough that HRH did not like her. Very few women made the grade with Regina. They had to be young or humble, accepting servile status, or be clearly *hicht geboren* with sixteen quarterings. She refused to admit any intermediate ranks. Two Industrial Revolutions and the rise and fall of the middle classes had passed her by. "Does she still wear a crown?" she asked.

"I don't know about wear it. She has one. I've seen it. Hanging on the bedrail. I suppose she'll wear it if they ever come to arrest her for murder."

"Do you think they'll do that?"

"They might. The case isn't closed. Anyway, for my money she's a murderess."

"My husband might have gone there," said Patsy.

"It'd be queer if he went there."

"He's on the run, you see," said Patsy simply.

"From what?"

"From you, from me, from himself."

In the evening the Grouts were in their living-room. Supper was over. Mr Grout was sewing leather. He had a skill of sewing and shaping leather pieces into leather pouches and purses which he then sold. You could hardly call it a hobby, as he pursued it with such an apparent lack of pleasure. He was wearing a thick apron and a leather thimble covered his thumb and part of the palm as well.

"Young chap across the road never came back then?" he said.

"No."

"Wonder how he knew the police would be after him?"

"Wouldn't be difficult to guess," said Mrs Grout.

"Sensible thing would be to have stayed put."

"Take nerve, that would," said Mrs Grout.

"Even if he's innocent now he looks guilty."

"I don't know about that. There's still the other one. They could both have been in it together."

Mr Grout got on with his sewing. His hands were moving fast.

Mrs Grout missed the danger signals.

"I heard you were up at the sweet factory this morning asking for Kedge." He didn't look at her.

"Who said that?"

He didn't answer. Instead he sewed a few rapid stitches. "*You* told him to go off. *You* did." His voice was getting louder.

"I never." Her voice was loud now. The cats moved away uneasily; they were expert at reading the signs.

"Liar. You thought Alf Bartlett would keep quiet. He did keep quiet. But not for long. I say you're a liar."

"Don't you call me a liar," she screamed.

He threw down the piece of leather. "You silly old fool. You'll have the police round here after you. You'll have us both in trouble. You think they won't find out? You think they won't be round here? What are they going to say, eh?"

"I wanted to help him."

"No you didn't."

"I went round to ask him if he still kept a key by the milk bottles. I told the other one there was a key there. That way he could have got in. He thought he'd seen a girl there. Perhaps he did see a girl there. We don't know who John Kedge had staying with him."

"Staying," said her husband. "You want to read about the way that girl looked. She'd been starved. Drugged..."

"I thought John Kedge had a right to be told," she said obstinately.

"You wanted him in trouble. It's the way you are. You've had it in for him and his mother ever since she called you dirty."

"She shouldn't have said it."

"It was the truth. As I stand here it's the truth."

They glared at each other.

"I bet you hope those two meet up with each other and one of them gets killed. Perhaps both. You'd like that."

She threw the contents of her teacup at him. He stood up and struck her across the face.

His hand was still clothed in leather and he still held the great steel needle. The needle went through her cheek in an upward direction.

For a moment, she looked at him incredulously, and then pitched forward across the table.

Chapter 5

ALL DAY Coffin was walking, walking.

He walked westward, until suddenly he knew where he was going. He was making, slowly and indirectly, to the oldest part of London. On foot and wearily, yet with some satisfaction, he followed the course of the river. He crossed a great bridge, turned sharp left and so came, at night but well before midnight, into a tiny square with a church and a stone seat beside a drinking fountain that had been new about the time the young Victoria was sedately taking her lessons in Kensington Palace. No water ran from it now and hadn't run for years, but it remained on the wall, its delicate shell shape and charming faun's head with open mouth much appreciated by those who knew it.

He put his hand in his pocket to take out a cigarette. There was a key in it; he took it out and looked at it but it meant nothing to him; and he put it back.

He sat down on the stone seat by the fountain and lit a cigarette. Comfortably he rested his feet against a black stump of wood which said this had formed part of the old Roman bridge across the Thames. The British, the Romans, and the English had all done some building round here and left their remains. No one thought anything of it, you rested your foot on a Roman pillar, sat down on an eighteenth-century seat and looked across the road to a building that had gone up to replace the one burnt down in 1666 and took it for granted.

Coffin began to enjoy his cigarette. There was one

lamp on the side of the church wall but otherwise it was dark and peaceful. Never mind what it was like during the day, with businessmen and messengers and tourists all hurrying about; at night the city rested. This area by St Magnus's Church was a bywater anyway. You could sit comfortably with the gravestones under your feet without it worrying you. St Magnus's Church had been a famous sanctuary once for wrongdoers and outlaws. His right extended far back in history, back beyond the day when good King Edward was alive and dead, as Domesday Book tellingly puts it, back into the distant days when Dane and Saxon coexisted uneasily in London. Once you had got your hand on the door of St Magnus's Church you were safe. Safety was your assured inalienable right and no one's justice, not even the king's, could reach you.

Something of this atmosphere still remained. Here was peace and gentleness. Coffin was in sanctuary.

The night wind blew softly and lightly with rain. The moon came out from behind a cloud and shone on the fountain and the faun. Not far away the dark waters of the Thames moved quietly.

He thought he was being looked for. "There's a girl dead," he told himself, "and they're looking for me." He could guess who were looking for him. He could even put a name to them, but their faces were gone. They were faceless. Strange but true. Perhaps that was how everyone on the run felt.

Behind him he had left some noticeable landmarks. The hostel where he had slept, the hospital. He scratched his wrist reflectively; the irritation seemed no better. He had walked fast up the main road away from the hospital but he had lingered for a long while near a goldfish pond in a little park, studying the report in the newspaper and staring at the goldfish. This pond was overlooked by a classroom in a local school. It was the art room, and the pupils found plenty of opportunities to look out. Several saw Coffin and at one point a group of three were drawing him as a 'study from life'. For a long time after this on the next part of his walk no one noticed him. Then he sat in a bus shelter to rest and read another later newspaper he had bought and a bus driver saw him and knew him. From these contacts some strands led back to the police and some to Alberta and no crystal balls needed.

Alberta knew better than to try to look for Coffin straight away, although once she had read the papers she knew she would be after him soon. There was more in him to use now. He was a suspected murderer, and suspected murderers couldn't be choosy. She didn't think for one moment he was guilty, in her reading he was not a killer, but the suspicion would hang over him. He had gone one step lower on the ladder. She read the paper over her lunch, which today was soup and fruit, prepared by herself and eaten over her work.

Today she had had a letter from Jess Rigby's mother and father in Newcastle. The postmark was obscure. It was a well-composed, well-written letter and fully explained what Jess Rigby was doing in London and why she was there, who she was and where she came from. As a letter you couldn't fault it. Her assistant had read it and exclaimed enthusiastically that it explained everything. "It does," agreed Alberta. Alberta put the letter and the newspaper into the leather case in which she carried all her papers. She put on a bright pink coat and a little lilac cap like a jockey's that went with it and painted her lips to match and then took off the lipstick. In her world it was very important to look like a girl who was too on the wing to have time to put on her lipstick.

"I'll be going out," she said to her assistant. "Case."

"Sure." Her assistant had got used to Alberta now but it had taken some time, she was so different from the usual run of women she had worked for. Prettier and smarter, for one thing. And something else for another. But what that something was she debated. The word which came most readily to her tongue was toughness, but that seemed an unkind word to apply to a girl who devoted her life to making other people happier.

"*Ciao*," she said brightly; she had spent two weeks in Jesolo last year. Of Venice, she could say, you *can't* go there in August, we stayed just outside. Lovely little place. Lovely little place for you and a thousand others, but she didn't say this aloud. Let them find out. Meanwhile she had *ciao* to show for it.

"Good-bye," answered Alberta.

Her assistant watched her go and their eyes met. Perhaps the quality she saw in that pale clear gaze was courage.

"What on earth do you make of Alberta?" she said, going into the office next door and speaking to the woman at the typewriter. "She's thrown away everything in her life that made it worth while."

The woman grunted, and went on typing.

"True, you know."

"Ah-ha."

"Oh, talk."

"I can't when I'm typing." She drew a rubber towards her. "*You* know that."

"But she has, you have to admit it, she's thrown it all away, husband, home, money."

"We only know one side of the story."

"She's an enigma. Why do it?"

"She wanted to do good in the world."

"Oh, is that what she's doing?"

"We all are here, aren't we?" Now she had stopped typing; she could not type and be puzzled at the same time.

"I'm just earning a living. And not a very good one either." She went to the door. "Bye. If I had a husband who devoted his life to making money I wouldn't leave him."

"Dirty money," muttered the other girl, bending over her machine. "I suppose that's what she thought."

"She's a puzzle," came from the door. "We don't have an idea what she thinks."

"I bet she'd be mean if you got in her way," called the other back. "I just bet she would," she said to herself, bending over her work.

Alberta had no idea they talked of her behind her back. She never thought of it. It was one of the things about her, loveable or hateful, according to how you felt, that she didn't care too much what went on behind her back.

She was quite confident the person she was visiting would be in, because she knew the pattern of her life.

"Hello, Jess."

"Oh, it's you."
"Not awake yet, are you? Can I come in?"
Jess stood aside. She was polite and silent as always.
"You're feeling better?"
"Yes. I could have gone back to work today. But the doctor said to rest."
There didn't seem much wrong with the girl, but no doubt she did need to rest. Her mind must be working overtime, coping with her problem. Alberta had to acknowledge that so far it had done a good job; she was clever, no doubt about it.
"Perhaps I should speak to the doctor?" she said experimentally, to see what the girl would say.
"No." As usual Jess wanted no interference. Alberta wondered if the doctor even existed. If he did, then he was young and gullible, or old and bored. Alberta did not doubt that he would have been carefully chosen.
She came into the small and carefully tidied room and sat down. The girl seemed to have an obsessive need to keep everything in its proper place. She had very few possessions (and this was entirely natural, whatever view you took of her background, whichever story you believed) but each one was carefully tended.
"Would you like some coffee?" She was already putting on a kettle. Anything to delay conversation. Her mind was probably beginning to turn things over. Such as why this visit? Did it mean anything? And if so, what?
"Yes." Alberta's mind was also at work. She always felt the need to keep well on the alert with Jess. This amused her even while it teased her.
"Just out of a tin," said Jess, warily.

"But talk first."

Without a word, Jess turned out the heat under the kettle and sat down. She folded her hands in her lap and sat waiting. Alberta knew by now that she would never make the first move.

"You may think there's nothing more to say."

Jess did not answer. Clearly she did think so. But she was unable to stop herself giving a little movement of the head. Alberta thought that inside her was a great pool of confidences and information, now dammed up, but which one day might burst out.

"But I can't just leave things as they are. You're a case, Jess, and you can't be left alone."

"Who made me a case?" said Jess gruffly.

"Well, yes, I grant you that. You didn't exactly ask to be made a case. Or did you, Jess? I mean didn't your own behaviour perhaps bring it on you?"

"I'm not 'behaving'. I'm just going on in a perfectly normal way. I have a normal life. I have my own life and I want to be left alone in it."

"You have your life alone now, Jess. Did you always have it?"

"No one's born with it."

Alberta laughed. Jess did not. She was never free with her laughs.

"You get it at the expense of other people, Jess."

"Yes."

"As long as you know that." As long as you know, as long as I know, as long as everyone else in the world knows it. We that have cause to know it, thought, Alberta, do know it.

"I've explained to you," said Jess patiently, "Only

you never listen, that my mother and father are perfectly willing for me to live here on my own. They are happy, so I'm not sacrificing anyone. Not anyone."

"And the mother in hospital in Wolverhampton?"

"She's nothing to do with me. Nothing. You've mistaken me for someone else."

"Yes. That could be, Jess." Then she added, "But you told me I would have a letter from your real parents today, all about you."

"Didn't you get a letter?" asked Jess swiftly.

"Yes, I got a letter."

"Well then..."

"But to tell you the truth, Jess, I thought you wrote it." There was silence.

"If I could just meet your parents?"

"They're busy, very busy. You can't expect them to rush to London because of some silly tale. Wasn't it enough for them to write a letter?"

"It was a good letter," said Alberta.

"It wasn't a good letter. It hasn't stopped you coming here."

"No," admitted Alberta. "Perhaps no letter could be good enough to do that."

"You're laughing. At me?" Jess didn't sound angry, only puzzled, as if mirth was so alien to her she could hardly recognise it.

"I was smiling. Really at your innocence. That you could think you could get away with it. If you'd only give me the truth I'd be able to help you."

"It'd take murder to do that," said Jess. And suddenly there was emotion in her voice.

"I know a man who might even be able to do that

for us. Or something near enough. We could stop short of actual killing perhaps."

"Where is he?"

"I'll be able to find him."

"You always seem to know everything," said Jess wearily.

"I'll see you tomorrow, Jess."

"I won't be here. I'm going away."

"I wonder where you'll be?" The light, sceptical question penetrated Jess's defences. She was silent. She knew she'd be nowhere else but here.

"Tomorrow, then," said Alberta.

Coffin sat in the dark, smoking. He was at peace. It was an illusory peace, but probably most peace is.

By now his old colleague and superior Chief Superintendent Styles had got it pretty clear in his own mind that the killer of the girl found in Spicerman Street was John Kedge. The police were now looking for John Kedge. Probably they would find him soon, but Styles was still looking for Coffin too. He felt great and continuing anxiety about him. He hadn't heard about Mrs Grout yet. No one knew so far, except her husband. He was keeping it a secret. The secret wouldn't hold much longer, though. The Spicerman Street story had been a short one after all (as Alberta had remarked of the earlier tragedy) and it was almost over. Just one or two little episodes to come.

In her crystal ball all the Princess could see now was that Coffin was walking into danger. She gazed anxiously into the ball but all she could catch was a great mist. She seemed to have lost her gift.

Coffin was a figure in a crystal ball, a man pursued and a man sitting smoking all at one and the same time.

He put his hand in his pocket and drew out the key and suddenly knew what it was—it was the key of his own house.

He sat looking at the key. A shadow fell across him.

"Hi."

Coffin looked up. "Oh, it's you."

Alberta came and sat down beside him.

"How did you find me?"

"Well, I followed you. I said I would. You've had quite a day."

Coffin did not answer for a time. His fingers were still playing with the key.

"I didn't expect you."

"Not here, not now, perhaps, but some time, surely?"

"No."

"I'm your employer now," she said amiably. "I've come about that job I wanted you to do." He did not move. "It wasn't an offer you could turn down. I don't think you realised that. You listened. You let me tell you. We're waiting now, me and the girl. You can't let us down."

A black car came quietly down the street, slowed down for a moment as it came to St Magnus, and then passed on. From where they sat in the shadow of the fountain they could see and yet not be seen.

"Police car," said Alberta. "They're not looking for you. Just looking. You know their way. But you don't want them interested in you just now, do you?"

"It didn't look like a police car."

"Not this time perhaps." Her voice was rich and

pleasant. There was something powerful and maddening about her.

"Whatever you've got on your mind, and I think you've got something," went on Alberta, "you'll be better with me now." There was nothing maternal, hardly anything even friendly in the way she spoke, but there was power.

Coffin got up and went with her. She had a small car parked a few yards away.

"It's not so late," she said. "I want you to meet this girl I was telling you about." She was a skilful driver and already had them out of this dark side road and out into the traffic and towards the bridge across the river. "You look as though time means nothing to you."

This was true. For days now Coffin's hold on time had been tenuous and limp. An hour, a day was here now, and now it was gone. It was one of his symptoms. But to some things he was very sensitive.

"You're from Wales, aren't you?" he said suddenly.

She kept her eyes fixed on the road ahead. "Once. A long time ago." It occurred to Coffin that she was displeased with his sharpness. *She* was to be the discoverer, but she was to give up no secrets in return.

But even a broken-down old policeman knows something, thought Coffin. "It wasn't so long ago," he observed mildly.

"I'm older than I look."

She was driving very fast, too fast probably, but the roads were almost empty. They were following the line of the river, going back the way he had come. Very soon they would be near Spicerman Street. Then they turned left into a street with a terrace on either side composed of thin narrow houses.

The front door of one of them opened and a young man came out and turned down the street.

"That's the house."

Coffin and Alberta went to the house where the door was swinging open. Once it had been painted blue, but now it was grey and dirty.

"This way." She led the way in and up the stairs. No one was about, but there was a strong feeling that behind every door was a pair of ears. It was not a house in which you could ever truly be alone, although you might be lonely. "Now my idea is you should see this girl and tell me what you think of her. Give me your professional opinion. I have mine."

"And what is your professional opinion?"

"She's either a liar who's trying to tell the truth, or a truthful person trying to tell a lie. Either way the story is not clear."

She knocked on the door, a crisp loud knock entirely in keeping with her character. After a pause the door was opened by a short plump girl with dark hair and black eyes. She looked sulky and embarrassed at the sight of them.

"I don't know why I answered the door," she said.

She eyed Coffin.

"You knew it was me." Alberta was already pushing past her. "I saw you move the curtain when I got out of the car."

"And now you've brought a policeman."

Alberta stopped and looked at her.

For the first time Jess smiled. "I wonder where you think I live. Of course I know him. He's a policeman.

Or a probation officer. I think a policeman."

She closed the door behind them. The room was tiny with a bed against one wall and a table drawn forward to be under a light. A typewriter was in use on the table.

"Been practising my typing," mumbled Jess. "Got to get up my speed."

A few personal possessions were scattered round the room. A leather coat was hanging up on the wall. It seemed to have a place all to itself, as if it was in a shrine. The leather was dark and gleaming but across the sleeve was a thin scar as if it had once been slashed.

"It's late."

"It's not so very late," said Alberta in a reasonable voice. "It's just that you're tired and nervous."

"I'm not nervous. I only wish you'd stop hounding me."

"I'm not hounding you, Jess. I just want to get you settled again."

"I've told you: I have a mother and father in Newcastle. Dad's an accountant. Mother has a shop and sells books. She's an intellectual."

"And that's what you don't like?"

"I didn't say I didn't like. I'm fond of them both. We get along fine. They agree I ought to make a life of my own down here. They're all for independence."

"They're not financing you, though." Coffin looked round the mean little room.

"No." She flushed. "But that's independence for you."

She had put on a new make-up since Alberta saw her last. She had painted pale green round her eyes and put pale silvery colour on her lips. Her own solid young face stood out beneath the cosmetics, undisguised. The colours were not for her. She would never be pretty in that sort of way.

"Anyway, they're not rich." She sounded defensive.

"They come and visit you much?" asked Coffin.

"When they can."

"They come here?"

"No. Not here."

There was a silence. Jess walked over to the window and looked out. Probably she couldn't see much. Coffin didn't think she was even trying. With her face to the window she said:

"All right. I don't really have a mother and father in Newcastle."

"I thought not."

"Don't have a mother and father at all." She turned round and faced them. "Just two old aunts."

Coffin sat down on the bed. Alberta stood facing Jess. There was no mistaking her stance: it was that of a protagonist.

"And I did sort of run away. Not quite in the way you thought, but I left them."

"Thank you, Jess. I'm glad you've told me," said Alberta gravely.

Jess gave a brilliant smile and left her window embrasure.

"There it is. I'm glad I've told you. I feel relieved."

"Yes, you must do." Alberta relaxed a little.

"Of course, it's not quite straightforward." She gave Alberta a bright look. "I haven't told you everything."

Alberta and Coffin waited.

"I met this girl on Paddington Station. She was

running away too. She said: You can have my name and I'll have yours. So we changed. I took her Insurance Card and she took mine. We wanted to keep it all straight. I became Jess Rigby and she became..." Jess (to them she must still be Jess) paused.

"What?" prompted Alberta.

"Jean Wood. I had the same first initial, you see."

"*Why* did you change names?" asked Coffin from the bed.

"Because I was frightened they'd find me," said Jess promptly. "They would do if they could. One is thin and always asking questions and has big bright eyes." She looked at Alberta.

"Just like me," observed Alberta.

"Just like you," said Jess vindictively.

"So now the girl we have to look for is not Jess Rigby but Jean Wood," went on Alberta.

"That's right."

"It complicates things. But I'll find her," said Alberta coolly. She got up to go, giving Coffin a nod. He rose.

"You understand I can probably check this. Short a time as you and this other girl have lived, you have probably left some trace on the records. What was she running away from, by the way? I can check on things like your employment record and your bank book."

"I don't have a bank book."

Alberta opened the door and they were about to depart.

"Of course we didn't exchange absolutely everything," said Jess suddenly. "She kept a few things and so did I."

A cold wind blew up the stairs and into the room.

"Such as that leather coat?" asked Coffin.

"That's mine. It's always been mine. We didn't exchange clothes."

She waited until they were almost through the door, then she said: "I shouldn't waste too much time looking for her. No. Not in this country. She had a passport."

"Did you think she was telling the truth?" said Coffin. He stood by the car. Alberta got in and sat there as if waiting for him to follow her. But he was by no means sure that was what she really wanted.

"What do you think?"

"I don't know."

"I think she's telling the truth so far as she's able, here and now at this minute," said Alberta.

Coffin closed the car door and muttered a good night.

"You'll want somewhere to spend the night," said Alberta. "Or have you got somewhere fixed up? I'll pay you in advance if you like."

She believes I'm utterly lost and corrupt, thought Coffin. I'm not so far off it, perhaps.

"I'll give you three pounds now and the rest when you've finished the job," she said, watching his face.

"Finish the job?"

"Yes. You haven't done half yet. What did you think tonight was? I just wanted you to meet her and hear what she had to say. Tomorrow you can go and see Mrs Rigby. Check what *she* has to say."

"She's in hospital in Wolverhampton?"

"Yes, that's right. Good mark for memory."

A strange soft feeling started up in Coffin, sweeping over his body and making his hands tingle.

"Look," he said. "I met you in a café. I met you there again. You offered me a job. I refused it. You said you'd find me when you wanted me. You did find me. What am I supposed to make of all that?"

She studied him without answering.

"What did you make of me? What did you think I was?" cried Coffin.

"I thought—I thought you could be bought. Have I proved myself wrong?"

"I know everyone has their price..."

"Not their price," she corrected him gently. "Their time. Everyone has their time for being bought. Tomorrow or next week you would have gone too far for me. Gone in one direction or the other. For the better or for the worse. Just now you are in the market."

In the house behind them they heard a window bang shut. Without bothering to look up they knew it was the girl called by them Jess and that she had been watching them and perhaps listening too. Voices carried so on the night air.

"You'd better clear off and go home," said Coffin, making as if to move away.

"As you've got nowhere to spend the night you might as well take the night train to Wolverhampton," said Alberta. She took a large manila envelope from her bag and handed it to him. "There's a railway ticket in there as well as money for expenses and the relevant names and addresses." He took the envelope.

"When did you put all this together?"

"Oh, earlier today." She sounded impatient.

"You were sure I'd be going."

"I'm not a witch or anything, I can't see events in a

crystal ball, but..."

"I once knew a woman who was a witch," said Coffin. The envelope fell from his fingers into the gutter.

"Yes, I expect you did. I imagine we've all known a woman who was a witch," she said calmly. "But yes, I knew you'd go."

"She could change her shape," said Coffin, ignoring the envelope.

"You have blood on your sleeve," said Alberta. "I should clean that off if I were you."

She started the car and drove away from him, leaving him standing there with the envelope in the gutter at his feet.

The train Coffin caught to Wolverhampton left Paddington at 2.30 in the morning. He had taken his time getting to the station. He had plenty to think about. So far all the things he was finding out about himself were disquieting ones.

Like the fact that he could, apparently, be bought. Not by Alberta perhaps. Possibly by someone else, somewhere. Alberta had just taken a nibble and left the main meal. But she had tipped the wink to any local vulture. Henceforth, as a police officer he would be at great risk. He knew what had happened to him. He had seen it happen before. A detective called Douglas Harris had been offered a bribe which he had refused, but he had known when the bribe was offered how it was he had looked to the world, and had felt differently about himself ever since. Other men had heard what had happened and afterwards had found themselves thinking differently about him also. Some bribes are an insult, some a compliment, and others just reflect your credit rating. Coffin knew which his was.

The Wolverhampton train was dark and mysteriously smelt of fish. Already, after only an hour, as it rolled across England, Coffin felt as if he had been on it forever and would be on it for the rest of his life. His compartment was empty, but farther down the train one whole carriage was crowded with silent passengers. They could be refugees or prisoners. Perhaps they were only people returning from a football match. They looked a silent doomed company but they might only have been tired.

Coffin, however, although the only occupant of his carriage, was not alone. Alberta was there with him. He could feel her forceful ambiguous presence beside him all the time.

"Hello Alberta," he said gloomily. "So I'm going off to do what you want. I don't know what you *do* want."

No answer came (although he felt her there quite strongly) and even Coffin was not so far gone as to expect one.

The train travelled forward, sometimes going slowly, sometimes fast. Although described as a non-stopping train, it did stop, and frequently. Nothing happened even when the train stopped. No one got on and no one got off, but there were strange metallic grindings and groanings as if something organic was happening to the train. Banbury, Leamington. Warwick. Soon the train would be in Birmingham.

Coffin slept. Alberta's presence had gone and if he thought of anyone it was his wife.

In the London he had left behind, in Spicerman Street all was quiet. The police were gone. The dead girl was gone, and John Kedge was gone.

Mrs Grout was gone too. She had died without regaining consciousness while her husband sat in sullen silence by her bed. No one knew whether he grieved for her now she was gone, or repented giving her the blow that killed her, because he refused to speak. He had said just three words since he had hit her. "She's done for," he had said to himself, and so she was and so, probably, was he.

After she was dead he loaded her body into a little van he had borrowed for the purpose from his brother who was a butcher and took it round to the large patch of waste ground by the Imperial Canal which was known as Harper's Tip. Lorries parked here, boys played here and dogs were always rooting around it. There was even one caravan. So it was hardly the brightest idea in the world to take Mrs Grout's body there. Mr Grout was not bright. He had been born stupid and life with Mrs Grout had not smartened him. He had the van drawn up near a large dump of bottles, tins and rubbish and was just decanting Mrs Grout when the policeman on the beat discovered him. This constable made a point of looking over the Tip at least once in a night. Such alertness had paid off before. Last time he had caught a West Indian magic maker, this time he caught Mr Grout.

Their lodger stayed on in the house in Spicerman Street, alone except for the cats, who increased and multiplied.

Farther south than Spicerman Street in the smart little house with a white door and white window boxes Patsy Coffin had received a telephone call before she went to bed. Her full name was Cleopatra, which naturally she did not use. For an actress the name was not an asset. She was a pretty woman, plumper than she had been once, and bearing upon her the unmistakable patina of success. Whatever had happened to her husband in the years of their marriage, Patsy Coffin had lost nothing and conceded nothing. Perhaps that was the trouble.

The telephone call had been about her husband.

"We lost him after the hospital," Styles had said. "He was seen walking away. Since then, nothing. But we'll find him." He thought, but did not add: And he had blood on him. To tell the truth, he did not know what to make of the blood.

"It's not a man hunt, is it?" asked Patsy irritably.

"No. No, of course not. But he's sick. He needs help. Wandering round London on his own isn't going to help him."

"It was what he wanted. He didn't ask anyone, you know. Just made the arrangements and went."

"He hasn't tried to get in touch with you?"

Patsy was silent. She shook her head. But the telephone didn't register that. "No," she said finally. "He ought to have done but he hasn't." She couldn't keep the resentment, even anger, out of her voice and this the telephone did register and exaggerate.

"Have you got anyone staying with you? Are you on your own?" Styles had heard the emotion in her voice and did not like it.

"I'm alone," said Patsy.

She didn't mind being alone. She washed her hair and manicured her nails and inspected her clothes. Her appearance was a professional concern with her. She slept well. She had strong nerves, but in any case she had taken a sleeping tablet. In this she was luckier than her husband. You can't sleep very well on the train to Wolverhampton.

In the morning, however, she found herself with a problem. She drank some hot tea and smoked a cigarette. The clear morning light seemed to have brought new lines to her face. Her hair felt too bright, her nails too shiny.

She was wondering, just wondering, if the house had been entered in the night—if some time between ten, when she had gone to bed, and morning someone had come into the house and quietly walked about it, moving a book here, a letter there, knocking a flower from a plant. It could all be imagination. Doors and windows looked impregnable.

She drank some more tea.

If someone had come in, then it had been someone with a key.

The train had come through Knowle, stopped at Snow Hill, passed Handsworth and Swan Village. At last it was in Wolverhampton.

Coffin sat in his compartment till a guard came and looked at him, then he got out and walked into the station. It was a cold wet windy morning as he went out into the town.

Chapter 6

IN WOLVERHAMPTON the Low Level Station lies down a slope in a side street, as if the original Victorian builders of it had been shy of publicity. There is a good deal of stonework about, and on a wet morning it all looks grey and unpromising. A lot of wealth and ability lies around in Wolverhampton, but this is not immediately apparent at a glance from the station. You don't at once realise that you are walking into an area that for energy and inventiveness and ability to make its way in the world is unrivalled anywhere. The city hides its agility behind a prosaic Victorian façade but underneath is really pulling faces at you.

"Morning," said the ticket collector. He was friendly without being particularly welcoming. He had a Staffordshire accent and a frown. He looked alert, bright-eyed and freshly shaved; he had probably just come on duty.

Moving away, Coffin tripped over a rough piece of grating and put out a hand to steady himself.

"Careful, sir."

"That bit of metal sticks out."

"We had two ladies do that last week."

"Then it's time you repaired it," said Coffin angrily.

"Torn your trouser too, sir."

"Yes," said Coffin. The small hedge tear did not improve his appearance.

He limped off. Perhaps he had hurt his leg a little too. By the time he had climbed the slope towards the town he was breathless as well. It was anger, no doubt. It didn't feel as if he couldn't breathe, more as if the air inside him was bubbling round and round, using up energy rather than giving it.

On his right he could see a small eating place just opening for the morning. A lorry driver was already walking in and the smell of frying was floating out. Coffin went in, too.

He didn't feel hungry, in fact he felt slightly sick.

"Coffee and toast," he said.

"Only tea."

"Tea then." He sat beside the counter and drank it.

"I do a good cup of tea," said the proprietor. He was drinking one himself "You're here on business?"

"Is that how I look?"

"No one comes here else," said the man with a laugh. "This aren't no tourist centre. We're business folks here and naught else. There's chaps here would cut their noses off if there was a good price going for them. So they say, anyway."

"You don't like yourself much."

"Ah, you're wrong there." He laughed again. "It's the way to be, I reckon. No one but a fool don't care about money."

He moved away to feed another customer. Coffin took out the envelope which Alberta had given him and which he had studied in the night.

The papers inside had got a bit dirty and he brushed at them. Alberta had done a good job. He had a high opinion of her professional abilities. She had Mrs Rigby's address (it was in a hospital) and a note that it was on a bus route; she had supplied the address where the Rigbys had formerly lived; and she had attached a short biography of Mrs Rigby. There was also another photograph of Jess.

A note in Alberta's neat hand was attached. Coffin had never seen her handwriting before but so that there should be no mistake she had initialled it.

This is a better picture of the girl than the one we sent before, she had written. *Don't ask how I got it.*

Jess was shown walking along the street. An easy enough shot to get. Coffin thought that Alberta loved her little mysteries; it was a weakness in her.

The lorry driver who had come in before him finished his bacon and eggs and went out.

"In again on Friday next," he said as he went.

Coffin finished his tea. His friend across the counter promptly filled it up again. "Here, have some more. You look proper starved."

"I'm not hungry," said Coffin, absently.

"Cold, that's what starved means. You know that way of speaking, don't you?" He took some more tea himself. He looked jovial and fat, blown out on tea.

"Where can I get the bus for the Fairymaid Hospital?"

"The Fairymaid? Get the number sixty red bus, not the green one. That's a country bus and you'll be in Shropshire before you can say Jack Robinson. Here, know why it's called Fairymaid? It's because the old man that left his money towards it made vacuum cleaners and refrigerators called Fairymaid. He left his money to build a home for old folks. They took his money and built what they fancied with it and the old folks still stay where they are out the Butsy Road, but they gave his name to the hospital."

He had a flow of more interesting information but Coffin had not stayed to hear it, he was already striding up the road looking for a number sixty red bus.

The Fairymaid Hospital lay back from the road behind a belt of trees and on a slight slope. As Coffin approached, a fine new building stretched out its wings in front of him. He thought that hospital building had come on a lot since he'd last thought about it. He really admired the Fairymaid.

He went into the elegant painted entrance hall where there was a nurse quietly writing at a desk.

"Mrs Rigby?" she said. "Well, it's still very early. I don't suppose the wards are done yet. You couldn't call it visiting hours." She sounded quite calm. "Still, we're very liberal here, we let people in practically all the time. I dare say you can see her. You a relative?"

Coffin shook his head.

"A friend?"

"Not exactly. More business."

For the first time the nurse showed emotion. "I'm surprised Mrs Rigby's got business. I'm glad she has. I expect she'll be pleased to see you. She'll be pleased to see anyone. She gets very bored." She was leading Coffin briskly towards a lift.

"She's quite bed-ridden, is she?"

"We don't really use that word any more," said the nurse, looking at Coffin as if he was out of the Ark. "It's an archaic concept."

"She can't move around though, can she?"

"Not too freely," she admitted. "But she's doing very very well, on therapy." There was a little cooing note of approval in her voice. Coffin felt he had a shrewd idea of what sort of note there would be for those who were not doing well on therapy. "We won't be able to keep her here much longer. We don't have room for her sort of case." She frowned. "It's a great pity."

"Some other sort of hospital eh? Can't do much for herself, I suppose?"

"Certainly she can." She looked at Coffin. "Mrs Rigby could go home, you know, if there was anyone to look after her."

"No, no, I didn't know that." It altered things.

Mrs Rigby was sitting up in her bed, looking cheerful, almost as if she was just there for a rest and would be getting up shortly to cook the dinner. She wasn't at all what Coffin expected. He had his eyes ready to take in a frail grey-haired invalid and she was a large well-built woman with a high colour; she didn't even look sick. Only when he looked into her face did he see a look of anxiety and self-doubt that he could associate with sickness.

"Jess was very fond of Auntie, of course," she was saying. "You couldn't expect anything else. Auntie was with us all these years. She really brought Jess up. It was what she said that went. Jess always knew where she was with Auntie. If Auntie said a thing was so then it was so."

"She was your sister?"

"My husband's. They were very alike. Clear-minded." Coffin nodded, as if he knew.

"That's the best way to be with children. Firm but just. And that's what Auntie was. She was very firm."

"She and your daughter got on well then?"

"Oh, there was never a quarrel. You couldn't quarrel with Auntie. You always felt she was right, you see. And then of course she was very fond of Jess and I suppose the child felt that. Oh, sometimes she had a little sulk, but never more. That's why I was so surprised when..." She frowned.

Coffin waited.

"When it all broke up. I could never understand it really, but then, there I was tucked away in bed and I didn't see it all."

"You weren't in hospital then?"

"Oh no." She sounded surprised.

"I somehow got the impression you'd been in hospital a long time."

"Oh no. I only came in here after Auntie died. I was took much worse then, you see. The doctors said it was partly the shock. I'd been ever so much better. What they call a remission of symptoms. You even think you're getting better. You aren't really, though. It's best not to depend on it too much, because then you start to go downhill again."

"And you got into this crisis at a time when you'd been feeling better?"

"You know, I like you. It's doing me ever so much good to talk to you." She looked cheerful. "I knew something would turn up this morning. I'm very rarely left to go right down, you know, without something turning up for me."

"I'd like to help about your daughter, too."

Mrs Rigby nodded vigorously.

"Right from the beginning I've felt that with all the people round me trying to help, they're bound to get her back for me," she said cheerfully.

"I should think people would want to help you."

"Oh, they do. And then, of course," she added

shrewdly, "they want someone to help me. I've got to go somewhere and someone's got to be with me. It makes it easier all round. So that is Jess."

"She is your only relative, I suppose."

"Since Auntie's gone, yes. We were all so close. At least I'd have *said* we were so close. Auntie was very good to me but she was strict with Jess. Of course, it's a good way to be with children, but after Jess began to grow up she stopped."

"It wasn't the way it used to be?"

"I knew I could talk to you. Jess does love things so much. I can't blame her. If you've never had much in the way of possessions you want them."

"And of course the things girls mostly want is clothes," said Coffin.

"Auntie thought if you had a good top coat and a dress to wear underneath it you had all you needed."

He waited for her to go on.

"Jess was a good girl about money. She earned it and saved it, as well as giving Auntie the housekeeping. Auntie couldn't work *and* look after me. At least she had to until Jess left school. Then Jess took over. Of course, she didn't support us entirely. I have a pension and so had Auntie. She saved that. Auntie was a real saver, but she had no benefit of it. Nor had we."

"No?"

"No. She made no will and all the money went to a nephew. Her dead sister's son. Not that I expected her to leave it to me. We all thought she'd outlive me. Auntie thought she'd live forever. That sort always go first, I've noticed."

Coffin listened. She wanted to talk.

"Auntie's way was right, of course, but it made Jess a bit secretive. She bought things she didn't tell Auntie about. Auntie always found out though. You couldn't keep anything from Auntie. I know. Then there was the boy…" She sighed.

"I thought there might be going to be a boy," said Coffin.

"I never saw him. Quite a nice family, I believe, but got in with a rough crowd. Auntie didn't care for him. You couldn't blame her."

They were eyeing each other now with complete understanding. He could see the picture through her eyes but perhaps he saw more of it than she did. She had unconsciously smoothed out some rough corners, he could see them entire.

"Plenty of room for quarrel there," he observed.

"They didn't quarrel in front of me."

"But you heard them."

She flushed. "Yes. Sometimes. Voices, you know. I knew both their tones so well. I could tell anger. The night Auntie died."

"A quarrel then?"

"No, that night there wasn't a quarrel. Only Auntie would go on and on about a leather coat Jess wanted to buy. The boy was there too. He answered Auntie back, I suppose. Anyway she told him to leave the house. Both of them went then. I heard the door bang. And a little while later Auntie fell down the stairs. She missed her footing through being so upset. I heard her go down. I could walk then and I came out of the living room and found her. Only I couldn't move fast and it took me a time to get to her and then to get help. It was too late. She never came round, poor Auntie. They said she fell awkward and fractured her skull. It was a very steep stair we had in the house. And there was a plant stand made of metal at the bottom on the left. She hit that."

"She did fall awkward," said Coffin.

Mrs Rigby shook her head without answering.

"Jess never came back?"

"I haven't seen her since. She wrote, telling me not to worry. No address, I couldn't tell her about Auntie. I suppose she doesn't know."

"I think she *does*," said Coffin. He had so many thoughts in his mind which she must not see.

He showed her the photograph which Alberta had given him of the girl who now called herself Jess.

"Ah, it's a lovely photograph," she said, smiling with pleasure. "She's a pretty girl, you must admit." She bent over it. "It really gives me pleasure."

"I see it does."

"Who took it?"

"I don't know. A girl who knows her, probably."

She studied it for a minute more, then handed it back.

"Yes, it's a good picture. Only a snap but it came off. But you're wrong about who took it. It's a professional job."

"You seem to know about photography."

"You've got to know about something."

"Is it your daughter?"

"It could be. It looks like her. But different. I have to be honest, don't I?"

He studied her face, searching it for some likeness to the girl he had seen.

"That remark you made," he said suddenly. "About photography: that you've got to know about something. Was that your own remark or were you repeating someone else's? It was your own, wasn't it?"

"Did it mean something to you?" she asked, amused.

"Yes, I think it did."

Coffin telephoned Alberta from Paddington station as soon as he got back to London.

"Yes?" Perhaps she was a little surprised to hear from him so soon. She was not pleased to have him take the initiative.

"We must go round and see this girl again," he said, straight away. "Together. Tonight."

"Yes?" She was definitely displeased now. "I am busy. It may not be possible."

"I can't talk to her alone."

"Of course, I don't suggest that."

"But I shall do it if I have to."

"Where are you now?" The tone of her voice had varied slightly.

"At Paddington."

"I thought I could hear a train. Stay there. I'll pick you up by the clock at six. We'll have to chance Jess being home. I don't suppose she'll be far... If not, I know where she goes."

There were two hours for him to wait but that wouldn't worry Alberta. On the contrary, if she thought of it at all she might regard it as having a definitely chastening effect on him.

The usual population was shifting around the

station. The man with two cases, both so heavy they stretched his arms down to the ground. The man who had just finished quarrelling with his wife. And the man with the grey tired face and the creased overcoat slumped on a seat, who was apparently going to stay there for the next hour, the next day, perhaps forever.

Three boys were walking up and down eating ice-cream. It was a cold wet day but they were eating great cold chocolate and vanilla sticks with enjoyment. Every so often they looked at the clock to see they hadn't missed the train. Their parents sat on a bench near by and watched them. They were their lovely boys. It might presently turn out that one was clever, one bad tempered and one (the littlest one) rather lewd, meanwhile they made a splendid family.

"I'm sick of so many personal lives," thought Coffin. "I'm sick of theirs, I'm sick of my own, I'm sick of everyone's." He wanted something impersonal. It was too late to become a monk, though. He rather thought it would have meant Patsy promising eternal chastity as well, and there was no chance of that happening.

Once again he saw the man with the grey tired face and the thin overcoat who was sitting on the seat opposite apparently forever; this time he saw that he had been looking in a mirror and the man on the seat was himself He was still thinking this over when Alberta arrived.

Coffin faced the interview with the girl sadly. He felt uneasy, doubtful. Somehow when he had started out on his initial self-search he had felt sure that the person he would come home with would be someone he'd like. Now he wasn't so sure. He didn't like the person he was discovering. He was violent, he bore grudges, and he had a long memory to go with it.

This made it impossible for him to be superficial about Jess Rigby. Various emotions about her and Alberta which he would rather not entertain kept getting in and presenting their visiting cards. Anger for a start.

It made him surly with Alberta. But she was not sensitive and did not notice. The hard aloof quality that had always marked her was very obvious now. You couldn't be what she was going to be, do what she would do with her life, and have that immediate sympathy for others that makes people sick when they see an accident.

"Well?" she said, almost gaily, settling herself into her driving seat and getting them out of the station traffic fast. She drove well, but the car itself was old. "Is the girl Jess Rigby?"

"Judge for yourself. The girl in Wolverhampton was a good, money-saving, hard-working girl."

"That sounds like the Jess I know."

"Yes. She was also a girl who could suddenly burst into an act of violence. The girl I've seen here looks to me like a girl that can hang on to her temper."

"Yes." Alberta frowned.

"In fact you and I know she can," persisted Coffin. "We gave her provocation and she kept her head."

"She has control," admitted Alberta.

"Mrs Rigby says her daughter is clever."

"So is the one we know."

"But secretive. The other girl who changed cards on

Paddington Station could be such a girl."

"If there ever was such a girl."

"Mrs Rigby says *her* daughter wasn't imaginative and didn't have a passport."

"What about the photograph. Did she recognise the girl in it?"

Coffin smiled. "Yes and no. She did and she didn't. She couldn't be sure."

Alberta drove quickly.

"Why are you so eager?" asked Coffin. "Just answer me that? Why are you so eager?"

"I'm just in a hurry. Events don't sit and wait for you to catch up with them. You ought to know that. Especially with this girl." He could only see her in profile. It was a beautiful face with the regular, slightly blunted bones of a Greek goddess. The eyes had the same remote far-scanning look to them: a Greek goddess with her hunting look on. But there was a wry curve to the lips that was probably not in the classical canon, a slight touch of the Gothic. It was souls this goddess was hunting.

"They're still looking for you, you know," she said suddenly, not looking at him but the road ahead. "The police. Your old friends."

"How do you know?"

"I've got my methods. You ought to know that. They want to find you."

"They can find me any time they want."

They finished the drive in silence.

Jess opened her door to them wearing a coat and a scarf tied over her hair.

"Oh, you're just going out," said Alberta.

Jess did not answer, just stood aside to let them come in. She had a strange look on her face.

"You weren't at work today."

"No," said Jess, making a long reflective sound of it as if she had only just realised it herself and was surprised.

"Are you ill?"

"No, not ill." She had a strained sick look which might have been pain. "I had things to do."

"You don't look well."

"I don't think you know how you worry me."

Alberta looked at her with sympathy but without weakening. "It's time to get things cleared up."

"You don't have any power over me at all," said Jess crisply.

"Power? What a silly thing to say. Who's talking about power. Power means that you can make things happen. I can make lots of things happen. I'm making something happen now."

"She's right there," said Coffin to Jess. "Are you sure you can take in what she's making happen?" He waited to see the look of understanding which must come into her eyes. It came. He felt sorry for her.

"You can't touch me. I'm me. I live in this room. I'm alone."

"You've got millions of brothers and sisters all over the world," said Alberta.

Jess turned on her with fury. "Shut up," she cried. "Why don't you make her go away," she said, turning to Coffin. But they had both come to stay, at any rate for the time being, and she knew it and they knew it.

"I don't see why I can't be just left alone," she said, but she did see, as everyone must in the end, and there was no conviction in her voice. Coffin was learning from her that all escapers suffer from the same illusions: that there was some magic in being alone. It was an illusion that you didn't keep long, because you soon realised that you wouldn't be let alone. This led to the other illusion of all escapers: that there was a great conspiracy against them. And behind it all was the first great illusion of all, of course: that you could escape. (And then sometimes you found you wanted to go back. Moved by a mixture of motives, you wanted to open your own front door again. His key was a dead weight in his pocket.)

Her tiny little room just took the three of them in with no space to spare. Coffin had to sit on the bed again. Alberta stood. Jess kept her coat on. For her it was nearly the end. She looked cold. But it was too late for her to shiver. She couldn't afford the risk a shiver brought with it of her being shattered into tiny pieces; she had to hold together.

"I've told you who I am. This being Jess Rigby is all a silly game. That was the girl on the station. I'm sorry for it now."

"There was no girl. You'll have to deny the girl."

"I don't deny the girl."

"It's just a formality. We never believed in her. But you'll have to deny her."

"No."

"In the end you will."

"I didn't invent her. I don't have that sort of imagination."

"No. So your mother said. But someone else did."

"What's that?" said Alberta.

"Oh you're surprised, are you?" said Coffin looking at her. "To hear of someone else?"

"Interested," said Alberta. That went without saying. Goddesses have to be omniscient. She looked a little displeased but goddesses have a lot on their minds. It wasn't to be expected that Jess was her only problem.

"I suppose he was a sort of magician for you," said Coffin, turning again to Jess. "He rubbed a lamp and changed the look of your world. A world you didn't like too much. I suppose you aren't old enough to know a lot of young men who could have done that for you. You thought it was *him*. You thought he was special."

Jess looked at him without any expression at all. She had naturally a self-contained obvious look and her life had taught her to mask her feelings. That was where her aunt had gone wrong, Coffin thought. But not her mother. Her mother had known that behind that composed face ticked a little time bomb.

"I went to Wolverhampton yesterday. I saw your mother. And she is your mother, Jess. You don't look the same but you talk the same. I noticed almost at once."

Jess looked as if she would never willingly talk again. "And I learnt something there: that on the night Jess left home there was a quarrel. And as a result of that quarrel and the fight that went with it Jess's aunt died. You might almost say she was killed."

"I knew the aunt was dead," said Alberta.

"But I discovered when." A noise escaped Jess and Coffin looked at her. "I think Jess discovered it today, too. I think she did some telephoning and found out. I think that's why she looks the way she does."

"How do I look?" asked Jess.

"As if you weren't listening to me. You're listening to something, though. But not me. Who are you listening to, Jess?"

"No one you know." She turned away to the window again.

"I'm not so sure. Where did you go today, Jess?"

She did not answer, but she turned round to face him again.

"I'll tell *you*, then," said Coffin.

"Tell us both," said Alberta.

"Oh, not in detail. Perhaps I can't give you names and addresses. Just the general outline. I think after Jess made her telephone calls today she went round to see someone. Someone who's been here with her in London, here in the background of her life all the time."

Jess began to shiver.

"Was he that pale-faced boy I saw leave the house the first time I came here?"

Jess hugged her coat closer around her. Her eyes, big and black, stared at Coffin.

"You're not imaginative, this boy looks as though he is. He was the one in the house the night you quarrelled with your aunt, wasn't he, Jess? He pushed her down the stairs. Perhaps he didn't know he'd killed her. We'll give him the benefit of the doubt. I think he did know, but we can't prove it. You didn't know until today. Then you went straight round to see him. Didn't you?" There was a pause. "You might as well answer."

"Yes." She licked her lips nervously. "Yes."

"What did you do to him, Jess?"

She smiled. Marvellously and terribly, she smiled.

"What's this?" said Alberta sharply.

"Oh, you surely didn't suppose she'd let him go unpunished?" said Coffin turning to look at her. "Hadn't you read her better than that? What did you do to him, Jess?"

Since she still did not answer. He went over and drew her hands away from her coat, she not resisting much. The coat fell open. On the front there was a patch of blood. They both had blood on them now. Coffin and Jess.

Jess drew the coat back round her and with dignity went to sit on the one chair. She sat on the chair by the desk and looked up at them.

"What have you done?"

"You'll have to wait and find out," she said.

On the stairs outside, Alberta said: "You'd better go. I'll take over now."

"You won't get anything out of her."

"Oh yes." Alberta sounded confident.

"Not for a long long while. She'll take her time. You haven't got time. What do you suppose she did to the boy? Stabbed him?"

"I must get back," said Alberta, her eyes on the door.

"If you'd left things alone nothing else would have happened. You know that? Look what's happened now."

"Keep your voice down."

"You intended it," said Coffin, staring at her face, calm and unsurprised. He was suddenly enlightened. "You meant it to happen."

"I thought there was something hidden. I don't like people getting away with things."

"I believe you're really a very wicked woman."

She shook her head.

"I don't understand you. What sort of a woman are you?"

"Ordinary."

"I don't believe it."

"My secretary and her friends make up all sorts of stories about me. How I was rich, had a rich husband, left him to devote myself to this sort of life. None of it's true. I don't know why they make up stories."

But Coffin knew. She was the sort of woman to attract myth. She would always be a woman who had stories told about her.

"I did have a husband. But he died. I knew he was dying when we married." She left it at that. He saw that she was not an articulate woman. She handled words stiffly and as little as possible. Perhaps she was lacking in imagination.

"That's not so ordinary in itself," he said.

"Don't misunderstand me about Jess. All the things I have started I shall finish. I'll look after Jess. She needs it. But it all had to come out first."

"And the boy?"

"It had to be," she said, her voice hard and clear. "I'll find out about him."

"She's probably killed him."

Alberta was silent. Then she said "No, I don't think so. But in any case these things make their own pattern. We cannot assume justice always wears the face we expect it to wear."

No, not a wicked woman, thought Coffin, but a saint. She was a saint. She had the hard unsentimental clarity of a certain kind of saint. No dove-like softness here, but force and certainty. She might have ruled a nunnery or converted an imperial province. Instead she was at work in south London.

"I suppose I'll find out about the boy some time," he muttered, pushing past her to go down the stairs.

"Be careful for yourself," warned Alberta. "You're in trouble yourself. You have blood on you." She said it sadly.

"It was an accident." He looked at his sleeve. Not even his own accident.

"Accident? You're violent. You're a man halfway to hunting someone. Have you looked at yourself lately?"

He did look. There was a mirror on the wall. His face was thin, with a hard red set colour on his cheeks as if it had been painted. It ought to have made him look very well, it made him look terribly ill. He looked a violent man.

"I am warning you," said Alberta. "You have to think about yourself What about that key you keep turning over and over in your hand. Have you noticed? You are always looking at that key."

"It's the key to my own house."

"Well, I ask you," said Alberta, moving away up the stairs. "Think about that. Of course it's the key to your own house."

Coffin walked heavily down the stairs and into the night. As if in response to what Alberta had said he turned his back on the area in which he had lived and on Spicerman Street.

As he walked he shut his mind to thoughts about himself "I suppose one day I'll find out about the boy and what Jess did to him," he muttered, deliberately closing his mind upon Patsy and what he felt about her and the key in his pocket, still warm from his hand.

One story was ending.

The only inhabitant of the Grout house in Spicerman Street, the old newspaper-seller, lived quietly there by himself for two or three weeks. Then one night he fed all the cats and carried them one by one outside the door and left them there. Then he took a blanket over to the gas stove, made himself comfortable, and turned on the gas.

Outside in the garden the cats called and scratched at the door, inside for the first time in forty years there was peace at last.

Chapter 7

THE HOUSE KEY was as heavy as lead. Was he really as obsessed with it as Alberta had said? But yes, it was warm, as if it had only just slipped from his fingers. He must have been handling it.

He stood outside a shop window and looked in. It acted as a mirror for him. He could see his face there and it looked all wrong, twisted and distorted somehow as if it wasn't his own. He had a moment's hope that if he walked away from this horrid reflection he might be able to leave it behind him. But he was not so far gone as all that: he knew he was not a ghost. He was certainly a compound personality. That much was true enough.

The shop was a hardware shop and it had a display of kitchen knives. Big knives and thin knives, fat knives and small knives, all with keen shining blades. It had never occurred to him before but there were many reasons for liking knives. They were such handy things to have around, to begin with. Five thousand years, more or less, of some sort of civilisation, and a knife was still the same shape. Its form could not be improved upon. All knives were beautiful too. You could hardly have an ugly knife. Only abused, ill-treated, broken knives could be ugly. A knife could help you live and die. For both this world and the next it was an asset. Which perhaps explains why Bronze Age nobles were always buried with their best knives.

A car passed in the road behind him, he could see it reflected in the window. From the car a face studied him. The police were still looking for him but did not know him when they saw him.

Coffin sensed the gaze and looked round: the car was already gone.

He walked on. The car turned, came back down the other side of the road and stopped opposite him.

Coffin stepped smartly into an alley between two shops. At the end he turned into a dark court behind the buildings.

"It's all right, mate," said a voice from a doorway. "They ain't after you. I been watching."

"How do you know?"

"They're after a man that done in a girl down near the Arches."

"That could be me."

"I heard they found him. Down in the docks. Hiding in a boat going to Australia. Trying to emigrate, I suppose."

He held up his hand. "There you are: they're off."

Both men heard the car drive away.

"Too lazy to get out of the car and pad down here. Them all over."

"And what are you doing here?"

"Here, here," he was reproving. Coffin still could not see his face in the dark. "I don't ask you nothing: you don't ask me nothing." For the first time he was suspicious. "Walk straight on and you come into the Lower Road. I should if I were you."

Coffin's eyes were getting used to the darkness and he could see that the man was very short, but with long supple arms and enormous hands that rested on his thighs. He raised his own hand in salute and walked on.

When he looked back the man had gone. A cat was leaping elegantly from wall to windowsill. Then it seemed to disappear up a wall as if flying.

"Cats with wings, eh?" said Coffin. "Or men like cats?"

He came out into a side street he did not know. He hesitated, debating whether to rum left or right. He turned left. One great block of flats after another stretched ahead of him.

He was in Lavender Fields. Once, when Queen Anne had been Queen of England, there had been lavender growing. And then after that a pleasant approach to London where Robert Browning walked before his marriage. And then, as Victorian London grew, it was row after row of slums. Lavender Fields had fame then, but no longer smelt sweet. In one January night in 1940 Lavender Fields disappeared in explosion and fire. When, after the war, Lavender Fields was rebuilt, it had gone up in the world. Several hundred feet up in the world in fact. Where once had been low roofs, now tall blocks of building stalked arrogantly across an asphalt plain. Everyone had central heating and a good bathroom. Adaptable and resilient as ever, the families of Lavender Fields were soon taking all this for granted. They still had as strong a sense of place and home as they had ever had, it had just got shaken up a bit, that was all. Give them a decade or two and they would have rebuilt the foundations of their society, and might even have created a new kind of slum.

Coffin, who had known Lavender Fields for thirty years, was lost now. He struck towards his left again, passing down an avenue between two great buildings.

Late as it was, one or two lights still shone in them. Even as he watched, one light went off and another came on.

"Restless lot." He thought he heard a far-away laugh float down from a high-up window.

At the end of the stone avenue he found his way blocked by a fountain without water and a high wall.

This area of the Fields was dimly lit and very quiet. He fumbled along the wall, down a flight of steps and emerged blinking into a brightly-lit side road.

He had come out within sight of his own house. There it lay, well within his vision, under a tree, one in a row of a dozen.

So all his doubts, all his hesitations, all his feelings that he was lost had really been a simple device by his mind to prevent him realising he was walking straight home.

The distant laugh seemed to sound again in his ears. He might be laughing at himself. Or someone might be laughing at him. People moving around in crystal balls must often feel there is a joke going on that they haven't been let into.

He walked slowly down the slight slope towards his own home. It didn't seem to be the right time to be coming home.

This was a quiet domestic road, lived in by quiet domestic people, some more prosperous than others. On one side he and Patsy had a plumber and on the other a young doctor. No need to ask who was the richer and had the Jaguar car and the new yacht. The young doctor said, however, that he was on the track of a cure for cancer and maybe he'd get the Nobel Prize yet, and that made him happy without a big car, and who wanted a yacht?

From where he stood he could see that both these domestic characters had their lights out and their families in bed for the night. So had Patsy, for that matter. Over there was where his mother lived, but she was away, had been for months, visiting her sister in Australia. She had saved up forty years for the fare.

The boy that Jess had stabbed was quiet now. His wound had stopped bleeding and he wasn't going to die just yet. He might not die at all if they found him in time. He was somewhere between sleep and unconsciousness. He had tried to call for help, but from where he was lying it was difficult to make his voice heard. At the beginning he hadn't wanted to call for help in case the police came. He didn't want the police. There was stuff in his room that would interest but not surprise the police. He didn't want them to find it. Later, as his voice got weaker, no one heard anyway. He could have got up and walked, but he didn't want to increase the bleeding. By the time it stopped, he was too faint to move.

Someone would find him. He wasn't all that difficult to find. Someone would discover him there. Sooner or later.

Bodies nearly always did get discovered sooner or later. Sometimes it was later, much too late and they were only a crisp of bone and shadow of cloth and leather which crumpled in the air, nothing to show who you were or how you came by your death.

But his case was not so desperate, since he was at least in a house and not lying on a moor somewhere. His body was clearly destined to be found. It was in the crystal ball.

Unluckily for him, no one happened to be looking in the crystal ball just at that moment. It was resting on red velvet cloth on a round table and by it rested a single rose in a vase (for the Princess liked her luxuries), and a crown.

The night wind blew down the steps from Lavender Fields and came scented with diesel oil and dust. Coffin stood watching his own house. In his mind he could see plenty of comings and goings to that house. He could see himself hurrying in and out. He could see his mother arriving, full of talk and gossip as she always was. He could see his wife. He remembered the time they had all seen her off on her successful tour of the States, when she had played New York, Philadelphia and Boston, then flown on to the West Coast. She'd been cheerful enough *then*. Come to think of it, surely it had only been since that trip to America that things had gone so bad? What had happened in America?

He could remember the day Patsy came back. She had come back thinner, smarter, with a new haircut, and very bright eyed. Presents, flowers and luggage were strewn all round her. Her luggage was clear emerald green and matched the handbag she was carrying. All were new. The hall of his little house seemed filled with a fresh air of luxury and success. Perhaps, looking back on it, he hadn't enjoyed it all that much.

"You had a good trip, I can see."

"Oh yes." She was enthusiastic. "So good."

"I ought to try it myself if it has that effect on you." He was studying her face.

"No. Not your sort of place." She was rummaging in her luggage. "I bought you a present." She dragged out a bright flowered dressing gown, the silk Italian, the cut Madison Avenue. "Isn't it gorgeous?" She held it up against him. "I love it."

"Mm." It was at least two sizes too big. "Plenty of room for me to grow."

"Yes." She was flushed. "Silly of me. But I can get it altered. Good thing it isn't too small."

"Perhaps I've shrunk since you saw me last."

"Yes, perhaps." She wasn't ready to joke.

"In your eyes, anyway." He tried the garment on. The folds wrapped round him lavishly. "You must have been mixing with a race of giants."

"Oh, I think so many Americans are so tall," she said vaguely.

"I'll start growing." He took off the dressing gown. "Miss us? We missed you."

"Of course." She bent down and hugged her son, who was detached.

"It got so I couldn't remember your face," he said.

"Oh, I am sorry."

"I managed." He was a calm child.

"Anyway, I bought you a present." She produced a large packet for him to open.

"Flowers, too," said her husband, surveying all her properties in the hall. He picked them up. Just an expensive little box of orchids with Fifth Avenue Florists printed on the wrapping. No message.

"Flowers too." She gave a faint giggle. Now, months after, he remembered the giggle.

That was the moment, he decided gloomily, that was the moment when the rot set in.

He slipped quietly towards his house. He was walking slowly down the road, but to him it felt like long slides downhill.

He passed the doctor's house. Everything all right there as usual. They were the family that bad things only happened to by proxy. They watched other people's illnesses and then got their immunisation shots against them. Disaster and sudden death were commonplace to them, but only in the way of business. Even the pains of childbirth were spared them: they had two adopted children.

A light had suddenly come on in the house of the plumber, Ironside, so something was up there. He watched with interest. Then the light went off again. The Ironsides were unpredictable. Although the master of the house was a plumber he had no control over the domestic equipment of his own household. They had more fires than any other house in the street and theirs was the dishwasher that exploded, sending red-hot knives and forks all over the kitchen. At one time they had even had poltergeists. In this one year they had had a plague of ghosts, measles and rats.

His own house was dark.

It would have been quite in keeping with his character if Papa Ironside had emerged at this point and said to Coffin: Sorry to tell you but your wife's gone away. He did not appear. This must mean there was no bad news.

He was a step nearer the house.

Some policemen deal with the problem of their life (which is that they must be at one and the same time men and society's revengers) by drink, others turn bully, some deal with it by becoming frankly second rate, they are the men for whom it doesn't matter, technicians without heart. So far Coffin hadn't become second rate. But there is a final solution adopted by a few, a special talented band, and this is to become a little mad. At the moment it looked likely that this would be his answer.

He slipped quietly down the path to his own front door. There it was before him, yellow and gleaming, just as he had closed it behind him weeks ago.

The key was heavy in his pocket as usual. He took it out. It felt hot now, as well as heavy.

He threw it up into the air, caught it, then pushed it into the lock. The key went in halfway and then stopped. He took it out and tried again. Again it stuck. He dug it in, pushed at it, then dragged it out angrily. He started over again. By now he was being quite noisy.

It did not go in. It would never go in and then turn and open the door. Therefore it is not the key to my house.

If it wasn't the key to this house, then what key was it? The key to the house where the girl had died in Spicerman Street?

I knew about the inside of that house, he thought

with a sudden pang. I felt I'd seen it. I had blood on my sleeve. Never mind if I thought it came on that other day in hospital by the water-cooler. Perhaps I was wrong. Perhaps I did go in and kill the girl. He felt quite mad.

Inside the house, his wife Patsy crouched on the stairs listening to the key scratching in the lock. She was trembling.

After he gave up the attempt to get in there was a long silence. Presently she heard him stumble down the path and back into the street.

Chapter 8

TO SAVE HIMSELF, to save everybody, he knew that he had to run. So he tried this for a while. Luckily the streets were empty and no one saw him. Perhaps a few people behind curtained windows heard, but no one actually looked out and connected the sound of thudding feet with him, this running man.

Dimly aware that he was creating nightmares in some sleeping minds, he dragged himself to a stop. There were enough nightmares going around already. Slowing down, his body calmed his mind a little too. But it couldn't be relied upon as a tranquilliser, and any minute he might start galloping again.

He looked about him. He hadn't run for very long, nor had he run wild. Apparently he had headed straight for the main road and had stopped as soon as he had gained it. There was certainly some sort of communication between his feet and his mind.

At this hint of a reconciliation, he felt strengthened. He couldn't be so far gone if his feet could reason things out. He walked steadily forward. Anger and fear were not exactly buried, they jogged along beside him like merry little ponies.

The road widened. Great buildings rose up on either side, which were new and shining and full of glass. But they were only a façade. Behind them the city shrank again, and the dwarfs could come out. The streets of little houses were white with moonlight. He was very near the river again. Not so far from St Magnus's Church, but south of it.

He paused. A police car appeared silently round the

corner, moved slowly towards him and then stopped. A uniformed constable got out. He waited.

"Out late?"

"Yes." It wasn't one he knew, and, almost at once, he saw that the man didn't know him either. Well, it was a long time since he'd looked like himself.

"Going anywhere?"

Coffin did not answer.

"Well, get on with it. Find yourself a bed. It's late out, daddy." He swung back to the car, big, and unimaginative, duty not unkindly done. He wouldn't make his way to the top, this one, but he wouldn't die young either. A satisfied middle age was already laid out for him.

The road felt different after he had left it. Not nastier, nor nicer, but as if it led somewhere. Not dwarf land any more. His visit had connected it with the real world.

There seemed to be a tremendously strong smell of human beings suddenly. The scent of living people floated up around Coffin. It seemed to come from near his feet, it was warm and bewildering. He wasn't against it (and not much for it, either) but it wasn't what he expected.

In the pavement was a grille of iron and this was where the smell came from, the hot steamy air rising up to his nose. But in front of him was only a blunt old wall with no door, no entrance. He walked round the corner into the next street. Half this street had already come down to make way for new great blocks of offices, the remaining half was deserted. Not deserted, though, he had evidence of continuing habitation.

Once an old railway station had stood here. Half of it still stood, and by it the entrance, almost blocked with rubble, of an abandoned subway tunnel. It was lined with cracked white tiles and here and there signs of blue lettering. Coffin could pick out a B, an A and an E but could make nothing of it.

He went down half a dozen shallow steps. A man was sitting at the bottom, eyes closed, sound asleep. On either side of the steps stretched a tunnel. In the dim light the white tiles still gleamed. As Coffin came down the steps the sleeping figure automatically drew its legs aside to let him pass. They were short little legs with broken black boots tied on the end, they seemed less like legs meant to be walked on than bundles hastily adapted for that purpose. If you took the boots off would you really find feet there?

Sleepers were stretched out on either side of the tunnel. Some slept sitting up, some crouched and halfway along was one who like a horse slept standing up.

Coffin sat down in an empty space and thought he might sleep too. He leaned back against the wall and closed his eyes. He knew where he was now. Although as an institution it had only been in existence about six months, word of it had got about. This was the old Backhouse Lane Station, serving a railway line which no longer ran. Soon it would all have been swept away. Meanwhile this tunnel, by some freak of London's plumbing, was receiving hot air from somewhere. Now it was a recognised sleeping place for those who chose for some reason or other to sleep rough.

He felt a sharp dig in his ribs, like the toe of a sharp

shoe. A voice, hoarse but feminine, and with careful vowels, said "Gentlemen on the other side." And then as, dazed, he showed no sign of moving, "Go on. This is my place. I pay ten shillings a week rent and my father built it. He was an engineer, you know."

She closed her eyes. By her side was a neat black case and an old musquash coat. Suddenly, she stretched a leg over the coat as if to protect it and opened one alert eye.

"And if you're wondering why I sleep here, then it's to protect my property. I like to keep an eye on it. You can understand that, I suppose?"

"Oh yes." Coffin humbly transferred himself to the other wall where there wasn't so much room. He wedged himself in between an old man dressed up like a brown paper parcel and a sleeper in a grey raincoat. In fact when he was over on the masculine side of the tunnel he could see her point. There were really two worlds here. On his side of the wall (he had identified quickly) you had a bench to lie on, ventilation from the grating into the street, no lighting or overcrowding. Across the way the light was better and only three women but there was no bench. The gap between them seemed enormous. So you had privacy. This was *our* world; that one was theirs.

Reassured, he fell asleep.

When he awoke it was already daylight and the man next to him was singing a hymn under his breath. The singer nodded briefly at Coffin when he saw he was awake, then went back to his singing.

The hymn finished. "There, that's done." The singer leaned over and spoke in a low voice.

"You get a good night's rest here. Not quite the Ritz, but good. Quiet, isn't it?"

"Yes." It had been quiet.

"And cheap, too." He was brushing his shoes and straightening his tie. "And the freedom. That's the beauty of it. You come if you like and you don't if you fancy somewhere else."

"What's it like in the winter?"

"Lovely, lovely." He had clear bright eyes that never focused on Coffin, who thought that he too would have that remote gaze soon. Perhaps he had it now.

They were not the only ones awake. A fat man was striding up and down the centre aisle shouting a series of orders.

"Wake up."

"Move that leg."

"Get your feet in, please."

No one obeyed him. It seemed doubtful if they even heard him. Each and every one of them had cultivated a special form of deafness.

Presently the woman across the way rolled over and picked up her vanity case.

"Can't sleep with all that noise going on." She yawned; took out a bottle of nail-polish and shook it up.

"Get moving there."

"Time to get up."

"Take that box outside, please."

He might have been a bus conductor once. Or worked on a railway. Or been in the army. Or just enjoyed shouting orders.

He barely got a glance from the woman painting her nails.

She giggled. "He's always trying to establish an empire. But I don't accept it." And she held up her hand to dry the enamel.

One or two people were beginning to respond to the orders now, getting up and shuffling their feet around or trying to move their possessions. Coffin wondered where the shouter had come from. Then he saw that halfway down the tunnel was a sort of recess and that this was where he had been sleeping. Either he had this specially favoured place because he was a boss figure or else having it had bred ideas of grandeur.

"He used to be quite timid till he found that place to sleep," whispered the woman.

But there is a long history to this sort of behaviour in the human race. It has its good and its bad side. Noah must have had more than a touch of it and so must Napoleon. Coffin thought that if he stayed here much longer he might develop it himself.

One of the figures stumbling round tripped and fell over. His hands stretched out before him on the floor. They were long thin hands with curving grubby nails and a scar drawn across the back. As they showed up on the floor they looked ready to be trodden on. He wasn't surprised to see a foot come out and grind them down.

He pushed and walked up the stairs feeling sick. He hadn't been able to identify the foot. He hoped it wasn't his own.

It seemed a long way up the street. Outside it was daylight. He leaned against the wall.

He had come a long way from home and got nowhere. He had set out on a long and, looking back at it now, a rather pompous voyage of discovery and had discovered for himself that he could be violent, dishonest, secretive and not above treading on an old man's hands.

He opened his eyes to see a young man peering into his face. He was the driver of the immense lorry parked behind him. He looked about seventeen, but Coffin realised he was hardly in the state of mind to get ages right.

"You all right, mate?"

"Yes." He added "I've just got over scabies."

"That won't kill you," said the man, puzzled. "You had anything to eat?"

"I don't know."

"That's the sort of thing I always know."

"As a matter of fact I do know, and the answer's no."

The young man put his hand in his pocket and pulled out two separate shillings. He grimaced at Coffin. "Thursday money. Always a thin day. Here—enough for a cuppa." He was putting a coin in Coffin's hand. "Here, you don't want to be proud. You should have seen me two years ago. See me now, sometimes," he added thoughtfully.

He waved his hand and was gone in a puff of diesel oil before Coffin had moved.

The shilling lay in his hand and next to it was the key he had tried to use. Now he looked at it in daylight, he knew its shape. It was the key to his own house. It was not and never had been the key to the house in

Spicerman Street. Last night it had failed to open a door it had once opened easily. This was a mystery.

In answer there were several possibilities. He would have to find out which was the right one.

He could see the back of the young man's lorry in the distance and it said in large clear letters THE PRINCESS TRADING CO. Without thinking what he was doing he started to walk. It took him all day to get where he was going but he got there in the end.

People who are swimming around in crystal balls sometimes get the message loud and clear. They don't have to know what it's all about.

Chapter 9

"AND ALL I CAN SEE in my crystal," said the Princess in an aggrieved tone, "are great big blue things. Like bluebottles."

"They must be policemen," said Coffin.

"After you. Running. You're in front."

"Are you sure your crystal ball is reliable?"

"Made by Fabergé himself."

"Yes, it looks pretty."

"My great-grandmother had it made for herself. We've always had the sight in my family. Or the women have. The men had the reverse, poor things. It made for very unhappy marriages and did the Crown absolutely no good at all. We've always known too much on the one hand and too little on the other. You can't get away with that forever."

"I'm glad you see me in front," said Coffin, going back to an earlier point. It seemed an important one to him.

"But you are in danger. I see you in great danger," said the Princess gravely, putting her hand on his and looking into his face. Her hand looked white and fragile, but the palm felt old and horny as he touched it.

"Yes," said Coffin, drawing his hand away.

"And so you've run away from home."

"That's not exactly the way it is."

"But it is exactly the way it is," she said sharply. "It is what you are doing."

"For reasons."

"Oh, there are always reasons." She sounded

sceptical. alert and not particularly sympathetic. "Some good, some bad. You look crazy." Now she sounded quite cheerful.

"Thanks."

"Well. I will hide you."

"I don't exactly need hiding."

"I think you do. From something. The ball showed it. Anyway. I see it in your face. You are, I think, a little afraid. Oh, don't worry. I am an expert in seeing fear in people's faces. I have had experience." She took another good look at his face.

"And what am I afraid of?"

"Yourself. For a start."

"Yes, that'll do to begin with," said Coffin. He looked round the room, which was small and plainly furnished. A dark oil-painting hung on one white painted wall. There was a small gilt mirror facing the window. By the fire was a table set with a white cloth.

It was so difficult to believe that the Princess was a murderer. But she hinted that she was. She was the genuine thing all right, of the Blood Royal. Not perhaps born in the purple, after all the true porphyryogenita is so very rare, but close to a throne on both sides.

She was pretty to look at, vague, old, and as has been said, murderous.

Coffin found her very perplexing. He had never had a royal murderer on his hands before. Alarm had tickled his nervous system as soon as he heard she was to live in his manor. He had, of course, received an official intimation from the Home Office and an unofficial one from an old friend, a retired ambassador.

"You'll find her an easy woman to deal with," His

Excellency had said earnestly. "She's a charming woman, charming," he added wistfully. "She made a morganatic marriage before the war—the First World War, of course, and he was a charming fellow too. I don't know what became of *him*. I heard she shot him. She might have done too. No one would have stopped her. It was a rough little country, my dear, but she had 'em all beat."

The Princess had once been rich and now was poor. But she didn't mind she said, she had always lived simply. Only later did Coffin discover that this simplicity meant taking one floor of the best hotel in Nice, rather than three, with an annexe next door for her servants. Now she was relatively poor, and lived in an antique house near the river, overlooking Pickle Herring Wharf, where an old London merchant had once fêted Peter the Great. (The Princess had no opinion of Peter the Great nor the Romanovs. "Everyone knows they were really Germans, not a drop of Russian blood, and, if it comes to that, none of Romanov either.") In this house she had set up her court.

It was a court which grew smaller and smaller. Every year one more old retainer or supporter died. A marshal, a high steward, a lady-in-waiting. One after the other they went. Was the old lady really doing it to cut down the expense? Every year, twice a year, at Easter and Michaelmas she still kept the two great feasts as her father and grandfather had done before her. On these occasions she wore her crown, now hanging on the bedpost. It was possible that over-indulgence in food and wine at these diminishing but still adequate banquets killed the old folk off But the last death of all had been hard to explain.

One of the Princess's most intimate and cherished friends, the lady always called Madame Catherine, had died suddenly after eating supper with the Princess. Of course, they always ate supper together, they lived together, so perhaps there was nothing suspicious in that, but on this night, the Princess had cooked the supper. Soup and fish. It was very nearly the only meal she could cook. Although she had learnt to make good coffee. There was no motive for the murder of the old lady, who was without money or possessions. But that she had been poisoned was established, she had plenty of symptoms and arsenic was found in her body. She had been getting increasingly quarrelsome lately, so perhaps the Princess was glad to be rid of her.

Now there were only the Princess, the cook, the former chief of the Royal General Staff and Her Royal Highness's cousin, illegitimate they said, still left. The illegitimate cousin, always called Missy, was an elderly elegant lady on very bad terms with her kinswoman, and it looked as though she might be the next to go.

"Hungry?" asked the Princess, seeing her guest eye the table. "I won't poison you."

"No." He was very tired, though. He had been walking all day.

"It's not as painful as you might think. I've made a study of it. Most people are resigned to it towards the end. Some people even welcome it." She spoke in a detached, matter of fact way which could not mask the real interest she felt in the subject. "People talk about poisoners. But there's a whole psychology waiting to be written about people who want to be poisoned."

"I'm not one of them."

"Oh, you might not know. Not yet."

The door opened and an elderly gentleman appeared with a tray. On the tray was a covered tureen of silver and a bottle of wine.

"Ah, General, how kind of you. The soup. And wine."

"Yes, ma'am."

"Over here. Serve some for our guest. You know him?"

"Met him years ago," said the General over his shoulder; he was pouring the soup. "If he'd had his way I'd be in prison now."

"I thought you'd forgotten that," said Coffin.

"Well, hardly. I'm an expert on prisons. I dare say your prison wouldn't have been too bad, but, thank you, I'd rather not."

"Poison and prisons," observed Coffin. "Two experts, two subjects."

"Eh?" asked the General, giving his royal mistress a sharp look.

"What were you up to, then?" asked the Princess sharply. "To go to prison here?"

The General just laughed.

"More soup?" he said to Coffin. "Wine?" He was opening the bottle. His eyes met Coffin's. She allows me my little foible, he was saying, she doesn't really mind. She is tolerant. She knows one must have something.

Coffin took some wine. It was particularly good, just as the soup seemed particularly poor. He could easily become intoxicated. All right, he let his gaze say silently to the General, I won't tell her all about what you were up to, although you and I know it was not all that innocent.

"I think I'm getting a little drunk," he said. He put the glass down unsteadily. "Don't let's talk about anything important."

"What to do with you is important," said the Princess.

"I never thought I'd house a police officer on the run," said the General happily.

"I'm not staying."

Both the Princess and the General smiled at this, as if, in their infinitely wide experience of being dispossessed, they thought they knew truths that Coffin had never guessed.

"We have good beds. Many, alas, empty now," said the Princess. She led the way to the door. At the door she paused and said in a low voice, "You will be asking yourself if I killed her or not. I cannot let you sleep in my house without telling you. I did kill her. I fear it is so. I am a murderer." She sounded sad and completely truthful. It was what she always said. No one knew whether to believe her.

"I suppose you don't mean that quite at its face value," said Coffin. This too was standard reaction. No one could believe she meant it exactly as she said it.

"I've told you the truth. I know where I stand. Take care you know where *you* stand."

The relationship between them was affectionate and friendly. With him she allowed herself to forget the Royal. Not altogether perhaps, but enough to make him feel unusual. He was flattered. Perhaps he reminded her of her dead husband. The one she had shot.

"I've lost the sense of direction lately," he said as he plodded after her up the stairs. They went slowly, the Princess was short of breath. "I don't seem to have been too sure of anything. I need sorting out. I suppose that's what I've been trying to do. You know how it is when you start to remember all sorts of things you thought you'd put away, and go on forgetting all the things that you thought would be part of your life forever. Good things. But not real any more."

The Princess laughed. One of those quiet little laughs that chill the blood in your veins.

"I am used to policemen. It happens to all the good ones, what you have. Unless they get shot first."

"I've had that too."

"So. You have been killed and you have survived. It is not nice, life after death. Now you know."

The house was tall and narrow with two rooms on each floor. One room was small and the other large. Nothing had been painted for years but it was well kept and very clean and someone had amused themselves painting the royal cypher at intervals on the walls. The freehold of the house was a mystery. No one knew whether it belonged to the Princess or to the descendant of the family which had originally built it. Some people said it really belonged to the illegitimate cousin called Missy and that she was the one who had all the money. It was very difficult to get to see her, so it was hard to form a judgement.

"Of course, you are protected here," said the

Princess. "This house is not under the law of the British Courts. I do not recognise their jurisdiction." She gave him a brilliant smile, showing white strong teeth. "Of course, it's never been admitted, but I keep trying. I have to be tactful, though. After all, there's the Health Service. I couldn't do without that." The teeth were probably false.

On their way up the stairs they were passed in succession by three people; a maid in a black dress, a tall lady also wearing black, and a young girl, each of whom dropped a quick curtsey as she passed.

The Princess smiled. "We have a small service each night. I say a prayer and bless them and then they go away. The words and arrangement are entirely my own. We left the Metropolitan behind you know. He was always suspect, politically. But we do just as well without him. You need not come tonight."

Coffin was not surprised that the Princess was head of her own church as well as her own state, he was only surprised if she was not her own deity as well.

"What do you pray for?"

"Why, for the Restoration of the Crown," she said, surprised. "What else?"

So Coffin knew he was right: she was praying to herself all right. To herself, for herself, and only herself. It was a fairly common state of affairs but the Princess had it clearer.

"I even baptised the cook's baby last week. Charming little creature. But very black." She added: "I was surprised how black. I suppose I thought it would be like a Siamese kitten. You know, pale at first, then gradually going darker."

She paused outside a door. "Here you will sleep." It was a royal command; he knew he would sleep. Drowsily he wondered if she had drugged the wine. But it had been the soup that tasted bad.

The room was small and quiet. A four-poster bed with embroidered hangings stood in the middle of the room. Otherwise there was nothing except a cupboard and a chair. There was an air of quiet mourning about the room and Coffin wondered who had died there last. He dared not ask.

Dazed, exhausted, slightly drunk, a very different person from what he had been in the morning, he slipped into this gothic bed and waited for sleep. Perhaps death would come instead. It felt that sort of room. But according to the Princess he had had one death already and hadn't won another yet.

He put the key from his own front door under the pillow and waited for sleep to come.

The papers were brought into his room with his morning coffee. This was served on a silver tray by the old cook. The Princess herself did not appear until the afternoon. He had heard that she held a sort of levée in her room for the privileged. Coffin wouldn't have put it past her. She was a tough-minded imaginative old lady who enjoyed exploiting the privileges of an eighteenth-century sovereign but who saw the advantages of living in the twentieth. For instance, the tray he had now on his knees had been made by Paul Storr the English silversmith (and how it came into the Princess's impoverished hands was a question, but she had her supporters). Yet among the newspapers was the *Morning Star* and he had an electric blanket over his knees.

The cook hobbled over and drew back the window curtain. He presumed she was the mother of the baby the Princess had christened. If so, she looked a bit old for it.

"How's the baby?" he asked.

"All right," she said gruffly.

"What name did you give it?"

"Electra," said the cook.

Coffin looked surprised. She saw this.

"The Princess chose it. Funny name."

"Very funny. Didn't you mind?"

"It was the Princess," said the cook, shocked. "Mind the coffee. Drink it while it's hot."

"Has she got a brother?" asked Coffin, still worried about little Electra. And for that matter her mother and father. He must find out what the Princess had in mind for them. It was an arresting name. Electra had encouraged her brother to murder her mother. But the cook was gone.

Early in the afternoon the court reassembled. There was no meal in the middle of the day. Whether from reasons of economy or to spare the cook for baby minding Coffin did not know. Anyway, he judged from the General's breath that he had popped out for his lunch to some place where the beer was good and strong and perhaps reminded him of rough bucolic beer when on manoeuvres in his own country. Didn't they do something funny to the beer there? Like putting rue in it? The General looked as if he knew the taste of bitter beer all right.

He bowed. Coffin saw that manners were formal this afternoon.

"She always keeps us waiting." The General looked at his watch. "Honour to wait and all that. Pleasure. Bore, too." He was getting too old to be a courtier.

"You have business?" said Missy in a sharp little voice from the corner of the room where she was standing. Coffin had seen her on the stairs last night. She was still wearing the black dress. Only now she had white gloves on too.

"You know Inspector Coffin, mademoiselle?" said the General. "Coffin, Mademoiselle Irene."

Missy looked straight ahead, giving no acknowledgement other than, a very slight movement of the head.

"Incognito, of course," added the General hastily. "We haven't got the police in."

"We have had… in the past."

The young girl whom he had seen last night on his way to bed came into the room, put down a bowl of flowers, and left again.

"Ten more minutes at least," groaned the General. "Really, it's too bad."

"Oh, you have business. I see it."

"Everyone sees it. It's no secret. Of course I have business. I can't live on air like you and the old …" Missy made a shocked choking noise. "Her Royal Highness," he ended hurriedly.

The door opened and the maid carried in a small black poodle, which sat bolt upright in her arms glaring at everybody.

As it passed the General he made a small growling

noise of protest in the back of his throat. The dog promptly growled back. They obviously hated the sight of each other.

The dog was placed on a cushion near a large thronelike chair, from where it sat looking at them, motionless and disapproving.

"Still five minutes," said the General. He looked at his watch despairingly.

The door opened again and this time the maid came in bearing a tray (the same silver one that had graced Coffin's breakfast) on which was what looked like a Bible. This was placed on a small table near the throne.

"Nearly with us," said the General with a sigh. "There is hope that today she may not be *too* late."

After the maid the next person in the room was a small boy (whose position in the entourage Coffin never got clear) and he was carrying a small footstall which he placed carefully by the big chair. He and the dog exchanged hostile glances.

"Practically here," said the General with relief. Indeed there was already the sound of voices. The boy went to open the door.

First the maid, then the young girl and finally the Princess entered. The maid was carrying the silver coffee-pot, the young girl a silky scarf, and the Princess a pair of white gloves. She only carried hers; the young girl and Missy wore theirs. The maid did not have gloves. Goodness knew how many centuries ago this bit of etiquette had been established or in what ancient story it was rooted.

In spite of himself Coffin was agog with excitement. She had arrived. The lady for whom they were waiting had come. She had contrived an entrance for herself, and with the meanest of materials, that would have done justice to Theodora entering Justinian's court. Looking at her narrow Byzantine face, he saw that she knew exactly what she had done and was amused at it.

She seated herself gravely on the royal chair. She looked tired this morning and her eyes were drawn and watery as if they ached. One long thin hand fondled the dog's head, the other lay beautifully in her lap. She never touched the book which had been so carefully placed at her right hand, never so much as looked at it and it was borne away at the end unopened to come back tomorrow. Presumably its place had been laid down for it about the time of the building of Versailles, when most monarchs were beginning to feel the touch of megalomania, and never altered since. The idea behind it, like Catherine the Great's rose tree, had long since been lost. Coffin never discovered what book it was.

But her pose told Coffin one other thing. All right, this was a joke and she knew, but no one else might laugh. The apparatus of the court might be a mock-up, a fake, but the Divine Right of the Sovereign was real. It was inherited, inalienable and only to be passed on by death.

Once seated, the General and then Missy came up and greeted her in a formal manner. Coffin stepped forward and did the same. He quite enjoyed the experience and felt he was the better man for it. He began to see the power of the monarch. Of people like Louis XIV and Henry VIII.

After this the Princess listened to some extracts from letters read by the General. They were business letters. This seemed to be her time for doing her accounts.

Then Missy, looking very cross, reported on the state of the household. On this subject Missy had not much to say, and from the bored look on her mistress's face, Coffin felt sure that she knew it all already and in more detail. As a royal person the Princess might know her place, but as a woman she wasn't the sort to let even a beetle cross her kitchen floor without being accurately informed on it.

The young girl did not speak nor was she introduced. She stood there with a slight smile, which echoed the Princess's own. After a while a faint but unmistakable resemblance to the Princess herself made Coffin ask silently whether the ancient position of Royal Bastard was not being filled in this court also.

They've got everything else, he thought, and looked speculatively at the Princess. Why not this? He smiled at the girl, who pretended not to see.

The General, having played his part, was now shuffling his feet uneasily, longing to bow himself out. The Princess saw this.

"I often wonder about that secret life of yours," General, she observed. "I'm sure you have one."

The General muttered something inaudible.

"Oh no, not that gaming club you run round the corner. I know all about *that*."

"It's not a gaming club," protested the General. "It's a select club for gentlemen."

The Princess smiled.

"All right. So you don't believe me. You can come in

and have a look. We have a Ladies' Night."

"The Princess can't do that," said Missy, shocked. Coffin had noticed that she always took a high royalist line, *plus royaliste que le roi*.

"Oh, I shall go incognito, of course," said the Princess.

"You might be recognised," said Missy.

The Princess laughed. "You may go now," she said, dismissing the General. She held out her hand, he kissed it and retired. Outside the door they could hear him beginning a hearty conversation with someone, probably the cook. Coffin wondered where he lived, whether he really lived here or only put in a token appearance and had a home elsewhere. This might be what the Princess meant by his secret life.

She was still smiling. Then she got up, crossed to the sofa by the fire and sat there.

"Now, let's be cosy."

The room seemed smaller crowded with women. Coffin felt out of place. He remained where he was. The young girl placed a table in front of the sofa and Missy drew up a chair to it. She looked expectantly at the Princess.

"Draw the curtains a little," said the Princess, settling herself at the table. She drew her rings off and placed them in a little heap beside her.

Coffin felt strongly that the trio were embarking on a well-known ritual.

"Cards, I think today, don't you, and not the ball?" she said.

"I always like the ball," said Missy.

"Ah, I have to be in the mood. Whereas with the cards," she shrugged. "They are less exciting but you always get *something*."

"We haven't had much luck lately with anything."

"No." The Princess looked up at Coffin. "Come and sit next to me. I'm so glad you are here."

"Yes?"

"Oh, very glad. Oh yes. I can't tell you how exciting it is to read the cards with someone whom I have seen in my crystal."

She was really keen. Coffin wondered if over the years she had gone a little mad.

"You said there was danger," Coffin reminded her.

"Yes. Some. We have to accept that. I have seen danger. For you, I think."

He nodded.

"The cards may tell us more." She beckoned and the young girl joined them at the table.

"Do you do this every day?"

"When we can. The General doesn't like it."

"He likes cards," said Missy with a titter, "but for a different reason."

"Oh well," the Princess shrugged tolerantly. "His family—it's always been their taste. His grandfather ruined them with his gambling. Whereas with us three..." she looked round the table. Her companions did not meet her eye, but their lowered bird-like profiles were, age and prettiness excepted, very like her own.

"You're all of the same blood?" said Coffin bluntly.

"Oh, we are all related in this house: one way and another," said the Princess lightly.

She laid out the cards and bent over them. "Something is coming our way, I can see it."

"Tell me what you see," said Missy. She was blind to the message of the cards. She had to sit there and listen to what her royal kinswoman had to say and to add her strength to that already flowing through the Princess's fingers but she could not read the cards herself. For her they played no tricks.

Coffin thought it wasn't so with the young girl, that she could read something, or thought she could, and was constantly uneasy at what she saw.

"I see a man," she said. "A dark man," said the Princess. "That'll be you, I suppose." She nodded to Coffin. "You have to believe what you read in the cards," she added. "You must believe."

"I do."

"No. I don't think you do. I can feel it in the cards." She swept them aside angrily.

Coffin watched her.

"You really prefer the crystal ball?"

"Well, it's more solitary," she said irritably. "And you get such tantalising little glimpses and you always have to ask yourself: Am I really seeing this? Am I imagining it all?"

"And, of course, sometimes you are."

"Of course."

Missy was quietly rearranging the cards. She didn't mean to give up.

"Come, Anna," she said. "You know we often get the best results when you have made a nervous beginning."

The young girl glanced from face to face.

"All right. One more look then. Yes, the same dark man. You can see him for yourself." She pointed.

"Only you can tell us what it really means," said Missy.

"So far it means nothing. We must wait." The Princess was dealing out more cards, distributing them according to a set pattern in a circle in front of her. She made an irritable noise.

"Why don't I go away if I am a disturbing influence?" Coffin got up.

"No, no, stay. Your presence is meant, I am sure of it. Perhaps we need the very disturbance you bring."

"Perhaps it is to teach us to be sceptical," said the young girl, in a quiet voice.

"I saw you in the crystal ball," said the Princess, staring at Coffin. "That cannot be chance, you know."

To his surprise, Coffin felt embarrassment and even a little anger. It was no pleasure to him to have been in her crystal ball. For the first time it struck him that the people involved in a miracle might not be so well pleased by the experience as he had always imagined. Perhaps Lazarus hadn't enjoyed being resurrected and Persephone would have preferred to stay with her husband the whole year instead of being dragged out every six months for the sun.

"Yes, you have certainly been brought to me for something. Now I hope to discover what."

"I'm not worried about him. I want to know about things that concern us," said Missy.

"I've told you," the Princess turned on her. "You can't share. I only see what's there. I can't put it there."

Although both door and window were shut a draught seemed to spring from nowhere and fluttered the cards on the table. Missy screamed.

The Princess leaned forward eagerly.

"There it is again, that card," said Missy.

"Yes, it's come again." The Princess was grave. "The two of Spades."

"That means something?" asked Coffin.

"Yes. It is death."

"I thought that was the Ace of Spades?"

She was silent, then she said. "It's a special form of death. That is how it has been for us. We need the Ace too, but that will turn up. You'll see."

Silently she recommenced dealing out cards. The next but two was the Ace. In between had come two red cards, both hearts. They meant something to her, Coffin was sure of it, but she didn't say what.

"So you have the Ace," he said, arresting her movements. "What sort of death does it provide?"

"It means death by poison."

Missy let out a long sighing breath.

"Does it come often, this card?" asked Coffin in a harsh voice.

"In its due time," said the Princess. "When a death is about to come."

"But you play this game often. Surely the Ace of Spades often turns up in company with the black two?"

"With us, no." The Princess was matter-of-fact. "It's strange, but that's how it is."

Coffin gave her a sharp look.

"And do the cards tell you who is going to die?"

"They don't give a clear answer," said the Princess evasively. She was shuffling the cards.

"What about those two red cards, the hearts?"

"Not decisive."

"Man or woman?"

"It means a woman. You know it means a woman," said Missy shrilly.

"I am the one that reads the cards," said the Princess.

"It meant a woman last time," said Missy in terrible triumph.

The drawn curtains were purple and yellow and the carpet had gold and purple tones. It was a royal room all right. The Princess looked at Missy and Coffin had no doubt her gaze could be fully read. There was a flow of inimical communication between these two women that bypassed words. Even the young one was the same. He turned quickly to see her quietly shaking her head at Missy.

The poisoned intimacy of this little court made him sick.

"Do you only tell these cards to see who is going to die?" he asked.

There was dead silence.

"My God, I believe you do. You play some kind of a variant of Russian Roulette?"

"No." The Princess leaned her head back as if it bore a terrible weight. "Anna, draw back the curtains." The young girl rose and drew the curtains. "Now, Anna, you may go. Missy, leave us."

Missy went slowly and reluctantly, she looked cross. Her young companion left with the same look of unhappy scepticism that she had worn all through.

"You see how it is with us," said the Princess, spreading out her hands. "We are a frightened household. So we are on the lookout for signs. Missy particularly."

"Portents," said Coffin. "Omens."

"You could call them that. But three people have died in this house. Perhaps by poison, most likely by murder. One case, the last. the doctors said they found traces of arsenic."

"But perhaps not enough to kill her," said Coffin, remembering.

"She was an old lady. Very little would have been enough. Missy too is an old lady. She feels she will be the next to go."

"And will she?"

The Princess shrugged. "You saw the cards."

"If they mean anything." But he thought they did. They meant a great deal to the women who watched the cards for signs. So now someone would feel doomed.

"You can understand we have developed an interest in the psychology of poisoning here," went on the Princess. "The motives, for instance. Did you know that the motives for poisoning are often ambiguous? Often the poisoner seems to have no real motive. Or perhaps does not know his real motive."

"I only had one poisoner and he knew what he was killing for: he wanted an old girl's insurance."

"Money is always a motive," admitted the Princess. "But then, you see, sometimes such a trifling amount of money is concerned that one has to ask: Was it really for this? How much did your poisoner get?"

"Thirty pounds. It may have seemed a lot to him."

"I expect he liked the idea of poisoning her. And then, she may have wanted to be poisoned. Many poisoners are fascinating people. Particularly to their victims. It almost seems as if the victim co-operates."

"Yes," agreed Coffin, remembering that the old woman who had got the poison in his case had repeatedly said that her son-in-law would be the death of her and yet had gone on eating the food that he brought to her. Food that made her so ill.

"Or at any rate submits," went on the Princess. "All this has interested me very much. I try to apply it to what is happening to us in this house."

"And can you do that?"

"In some ways. Not so much as you might think. We are a very strange household. I think I might call it unique."

"You called yourself a murderer," said Coffin.

"Oh I do."

"Well, then..."

"I accept all the guilt for what happens in my household."

"That's no answer."

"I have great guilt," she said simply. "I accept it. It is my historic destiny."

Coffin was baffled. She seemed to accept personal guilt with one hand and then render it anonymous with the other. Styles had had this treatment and could have told Coffin how it felt.

"There is one problem which remains in every household which contains a poisoner," pointed out Coffin.

"What is that?"

"Where does the poison come from?" said Coffin simply.

"Oh, we have that," said the Princess.

"I'm a little out of touch with police routine," said Coffin. "It seems far away. But in the days when it mattered to me I seem to remember that access to poison was what counted."

"We all have access."

Coffin put his hands to his head.

"You are confused," said the Princess. "It is part of your condition. I have been in hiding myself. It confuses the mind."

"Not confused. Hopeless perhaps, but not confused. I had news today."

"Here? Bad news?"

"Not bad. But something I wanted to know." He showed her the passage in the newspaper he had read over his breakfast.

"The young man found stabbed in his basement flat in South London is out of danger, a hospital bulletin reports. But doctors say he may be paralysed."

"Not good news for him," said the Princess. "You know him?"

"I know who stabbed him."

"Was it you?"

"No." He was surprised. "Why do you say that?"

"There was violence all round you in the crystal. I could see. Waves of it breaking all round you." She leaned forward to stare earnestly in his face. "It may yet be in store for you. I give you sanctuary here, but it may not last."

"I don't want it to."

"No. I can see that. You want to satisfy this violence that is in you."

"No. I'll keep it back if I can." I don't want to kill my

wife, was his quiet thought, or batter her or otherwise maim her, but I may find myself doing it.

"It may come popping out without asking."

She knew all about how you felt when you somehow slipped outside the group. Violence was one reaction. Her own had been to act like a queen bee and set up a new hive. But she was beginning to see that the violence had been built in from the beginning.

She got up and went to an old walnut desk. Over her shoulder she said: "I will show you what I have never shown anyone."

Coffin waited.

The Princess unlocked the desk and then unlocked a small inner drawer. From this drawer she took a square silver and gilt box decorated with enamels. She came back and sat down by him with the box in her lap.

"No one can open this but me." Her fingers were moving delicately over the raised pattern. "My grandfather gave it to my grandmother, my father gave it to me. It has never been out of my hands." She had found the spring and the lid sprang back. She took out a tiny packet and handed it to him.

Coffin took it. The packet was about six inches square and wrapped in yellowing paper. The paper was dry and brittle. There was some faded writing on the packet.

"How long have you had this?"

The Princess shrugged.

"It's been around the world for a long time." He examined the writing. In a fine delicate female hand it said:

ARSENIC: POISON POUR LES CHATS.

"Arsenic—poison for cats!" He looked up in surprise. "Where did you get this?"

"I found it."

"Where? Where did you find it?"

"Here. In this house. It was on the top shelf of a cupboard outside the kitchen. No one would think of looking."

"Why did you think of looking?"

"It's the place for secrets, isn't it? The top shelf of a high cupboard in a household where all the women are rather short. And old. Yes, it was the place to look."

"Where did it come from? Have you any ideas? Do you recognise the handwriting?"

"I think we brought it with us."

"With you? From your home? Your own country?"

"I think it came with us when we set out from the Palace. We were to bring some possessions with us. Many of us had a good deal of luggage. And then of course we were a much larger court. There was my father and his entourage, there was me and my ladies. Any one of about thirty people could have brought it out."

"I don't know how you can be sure." He was turning the packet over in his hands.

"You asked me if I recognised the writing. I do recognise the writing."

He waited for her to go on.

"It is my mother's writing."

"Well, *she's* not doing the poisoning," said Coffin brutally.

He poked at the packet, which was stiff with age.

"But this has never been opened," he said, looking at her.

"No."

"We don't even know if it contains arsenic."

"I think there was another packet."

"Oh, you do, do you?"

"I think we may have several more packets," she said carefully.

"All labelled *Arsenic: Poison for Cats*? All in your mother's handwriting?"

"No." She flushed. "There is one in Missy's room. At the back of a cupboard."

"And you left it there?"

"She may know it is there."

"By God, I'd have had it out."

"I'm not frightened of Missy."

"And that is the lot?"

"I have discovered one or two other packets. One in a hat box belonging to little Anna. One in a drawer belonging to the old Countess. She died. I found it after she died. *That* had been opened. There was another hidden in her glove box. Open, too."

"Has this house ever been searched? Did the police look here for poison?"

"They asked to be allowed to look after the Countess died. I let them. They found nothing."

"I wonder why not?"

"I suppose the packets weren't there then."

"How long have you been searching?"

"Months," said the Princess simply. "I look all the time. I am curious."

"And do you think you have them all now?"

The Princess shrugged. "The peasants eat arsenic as a tonic in my country. It wouldn't have been hard to come by a lot."

Years ago in another country a poor primitive peasantry had bolstered up its vitality by eating arsenic. They had gone about with the garlic-scented breath of the habitual arsenic eater. It cleared their skin and gave them energy. At the centre of the country the tiny court famous for its rigid etiquette and wild ways laughed at the arsenic eaters, imported German music masters and French scent and English doctors, but apparently lined its pockets with packets of arsenic. The poison had come with them into exile. For a long time it had rested, and now, years later, it was going quietly about its business again.

"The whole house is alive with arsenic. Do you keep any cats?"

"No."

"Someone told them."

"I don't like cats. All my family—we fear them."

A gong, gently beaten, sounded outside.

"Tea," said the Princess, rising. "We always have tea now. We find it refreshing at this hour of the afternoon."

Tea was laid in a salon on the first floor. Although this was a very English house it was impossible to call this room a drawing-room. Along one wall was a great gilt mirror, a huge portrait of a man on a horse filled another wall, a fire burnt in a basket grate. The chairs and the sofa were of some pale wood, highly polished, and upholstered in yellow damask. The air was scented with herbs and wax polish.

Coffin slipped awkwardly on the glistening wooden floor. Two oval carpets filled the centre of the room.

"Sit down," said the Princess, seating herself behind

a tray with two silver teapots and a kettle over a little spirit lamp. It was a charming, archaic sight and Coffin had never seen anything like it before. "You will take tea? Will you have Indian or China? Or you may have camomile if you prefer."

"Indian."

"We always keep camomile for Missy. Only Missy takes the camomile." She gave Missy a fairly malevolent glance.

"Did you bring all this stuff with you?" said Coffin, taking his tea and going to look at the picture.

"No. This entire room was a gift."

"A handsome one."

"There are still some people who do not like to see my father's daughter want for anything," said the Princess.

"I see." And he did. He had often wondered (and so had a lot of other people) how the Princess managed. She kept up some state here, after all. What did she do it on? Now he thought he knew. To use her own phrase, there were still some people who did not like to see her father's daughter want for anything. There was no royalist movement as such back in her own country. The peasants seemed as happy or unhappy with the new régime as they had been with the old. He had heard that the arsenic eating was now forbidden on the grounds that a worker in a well-organised state had no need of artificial stimulants and this had caused grave discontent, but no one had ever mentioned getting the old ruling house back. So the money didn't come from there, even if there had been any money in the old country to send. But emigrants from her kingdom had long been settled in England and America, and it must be from this group that the money came. They were known to have old-fashioned loyalist ideas. They also had one of the best organised criminal set-ups in the world and were reputed to be able to give the Mafia ideas.

He looked at the Princess pouring tea from a silver pot into delicate old cups. She was wearing a silk dress and her hair was prettily dressed. Even Missy looked as if her clothes had cost money. All this was being kept up on money derived from armed robbery, blackmail and fraud. He shook his head.

"Some more sugar for your tea?" asked Missy. "English people like so much sugar in their tea, I know." She sipped her camomile tea delicately. Her smile was fixed and tired, but her composure was as great as the Princess's.

"No, the tea's fine."

"You don't seem to be enjoying yours very much," said the Princess.

"It's a little hot, ma'am." Missy took another tiny sip, then, as if taking courage, a larger drink.

"Have a little more," said the Princess.

"No, I won't. Thank you."

"Oh do, I can see you are thirsty."

"My throat is certainly a little parched. I don't find the tea helps, though."

"Oh, but camomile is so refreshing."

"This doesn't seem to be." Nevertheless she submitted to having her cup filled and drinking it. There was something definitely unfriendly in the Princess's manner to her.

Missy was making heavy weather of her tea.

"I shouldn't drink it," said Coffin. He thought she was being bullied.

"Oh, Missy likes it really, don't you, Missy?" said the Princess.

"I believe I do."

"It's very good for her. She enjoys it."

Missy drained her cup.

Coffin thought it must have been a bitter brew.

His own tea was delicious. Just what his mother, that connoisseur of tea, would have called 'a good cup'. She judged her friends by the tea they made. "Fanny makes a good cup of tea," she would say judicially. Or, "I can't stand Alice's tea. She never warms the pot." His wife. Patsy, did not make a good cup of tea.

Was it likely she would, when you thought about her own life? Her father a drunken old actor and her mother dead when she was ten? Who was to teach her to make a good cup of tea? Perhaps the landladies of England during her time as an itinerant actress? Only they hadn't. Now she was more successful in her career (beginning to be *very* successful) and was married and still couldn't make a cup of tea. A totally unsuitable wife for a policeman, would you say?

He took some more of his tea. He certainly wasn't the best sort of husband for Patsy, was he? With this bag of violence inside him slowly becoming untied. It was just as well he hadn't got into the house last night. He might have hurt her. In one way or another he certainly would have.

"What's camomile tea taste like?" he asked. "I think I'll try some."

"Oh, you wouldn't like it. We only keep it for Missy."

"I'd like to taste it."

"I'm so sorry. I've just drained the pot filling this last cup for Missy." The Princess gave him a radiant smile.

"The last cup will be so bitter and strong, ma'am. I'd rather not." She was reluctant.

"It is a little bitter, but you know it will do you so much good," said the Princess persuasively. There was a white line round her mouth and Missy didn't look too well either. "She is a little bit of a hypochondriac," the Princess said in a low voice to Coffin, which was yet perfectly audible to Missy.

"No, I'm not," said Missy.

"I have to keep an eye on her."

"Don't," said Coffin; he couldn't bear to see Missy tortured.

"Just take it, Missy." She held out the cup. "Drink it."

"Don't," said Coffin. "Don't drink it." He stood up.

"Well, you *can* stop her drinking it," observed the Princess calmly. "But Missy *will* drink this cup. If not now, then some time in the future."

Missy took the cup and drank it down. She coughed.

Anna silently gave her some water to drink.

"Does she always eat and drink exactly as the Princess orders?" he asked Anna when the Princess was pouring a saucer of milk for her dog.

"No. Of course not. It has never happened like this before. Not exactly like this." She sounded disconcerted. "We all do what the Princess says, of course. She has power over us."

"She's a sick old woman," said Coffin bluntly.

"Yes, I know." There was no surprise in her voice. She too saw the symptoms. They eyed each other.

"You think of this as a sanctuary," said the girl sadly. "It is not, We are beleaguered. We are like a city that is waiting to fall. Have you ever been poisoned?"

"No."

"I have. I got a little dose once. I got better. Perhaps I may not get better next time."

"You mustn't talk like that." He was shocked.

"I hope you don't find the room too close, Mr Coffin," said the Princess, over the head of her pet dog, which was on her lap.

"Oh no."

"I'm afraid it is rather warm."

Missy was sitting back in her upright chair, her hands gripped tightly in her lap. Coffin could see the muscles on her wrists.

"Missy, you look as if you find it too warm," said the Princess. "Anna, open a window."

"I believe she's ill," said Anna, getting up at once.

"I have a little pain."

"Missy," cried the Princess.

"Pain," said Missy. She forced the words through her lips. "Burns."

Anna bent over her. Missy swayed and her head rolled back.

"My throat," she said.

"It burns and irritates," said Anna, raising her head and looking straight at the Princess. "Drink some cream, Missy," she said urgently. "Drink some cream."

Missy only moaned.

"She's past that sort of remedy," said Coffin, feeling

Missy's pulse. It was irregular and rapid.

"But it would stop the stomach absorbing the poison." Anna was bending over the old woman.

"She can't drink it."

The Princess was already at the telephone. Her hand trembled as she called the doctor.

Coffin carried Missy to her room. She was beyond walking. She moaned all the time as they went up the stairs. He found she was very light, hardly any weight at all. To his surprise he saw that she was wearing a delicate gold and diamond necklace underneath her black dress.

"Don't touch that tray or the cups or anything," he called back over his shoulder.

He put her down on a narrow high white bed. Anna wrapped blankets around.

"I will manage now," she said in a tense voice. "I have helped before. I know what to do."

Coffin looked back. Missy lay on the bed. The terrible thing was that he could have sworn that even in her agony there was a faint smile on her lips.

There was no one but the dog in the yellow satin decorated room when he went back to it.

He went over to the tray and sniffed at the cup Missy had used. There was no smell. At the bottom of the cup was a little sediment. He took the pot which had contained camomile tea to the window and studied it. He fancied he could see a little sediment there too. Shaking his head, he put the pot back on the tray.

If he left it, would it be washed away by secretive hands? He decided to sit there and wait to see who was first in the room.

He thought about the look on Missy's face. She was smiling in her pain.

Outside he heard voices and then heavy feet going up the stairs. The doctor probably. The rest of the house remained quiet.

There is something special about a house where a poisoner lives. It is secret and shy and full of selfishness. Poisoners are the sort that would walk on anyone's face to pick themselves a flower. It was possible, just possible, though Coffin did not readily admit this, that you might know a noble murderer but you could never know a noble poisoner. They were all rank bad weeds.

He walked to the window and looked out. He could see the top of St Magnus's Church. Not far away, as the crow flies, was the house where Seddon had poisoned Miss Barrow. To the south was the suburban house where a whole family had been poisoned off. One after the other, in a row. No one ever knew who did that.

On a table by the window was a square wooden box. It was made of polished rosewood with a complicated and unreadable set of initials marked out on it in gold. This box was old and much worn.

He opened the lid. Inside was a cloth of dark blue velvet just as old as the box. He lifted it. Beneath in a glitter of diamonds was a crown. Oddly enough it looked quite tiny, not at all as big as he had expected.

He lifted it out and it sat quite lightly in his hand. So one of the stories about the Princess was true. She did have a crown and perhaps she did wear it in private.

"It is only a wedding crown," said a voice from the

door. The Princess came in. "Not the imperial crown, that is kept in my bedroom. What you are holding is the sort of crown we wear on our wedding day. Bride and groom exchange crowns, you know. It's small and relatively valueless."

"A crown is always a crown," said Coffin.

"It is a symbol," she said proudly.

"Yes, that's what I meant." He started to put it back in its box.

"No. I want it."

He turned in surprise. It seemed no time for a crown wearing. Perhaps Styles was right in his joke that Her Royal Highness would wear the crown when he arrested her.

"For Missy."

"How is she?" He hesitated to put into words what he really meant, which was: When will she die?

The Princess shrugged.

"Why did you make her drink the tea?"

"Missy knew what she was doing when she took it."

"You poisoned her."

The Princess was silent.

"Don't tell me she wanted to be poisoned," cried Coffin. "Are you all as mad as cats here?"

"She did want to be poisoned. You saw for yourself." A faint smile was on her pale lips. The crown rested on one hand.

"You told me you were a murderer. Why did you call yourself that?"

"I am the source of all law, all justice in this house," she said sombrely.

"But do you mean that you actually and with your own hands administered poison to all these people?"

Anna appeared at the door, looking scared.

"I am coming," said the Princess. But she swayed and looked white. Coffin put out an arm. She did not refuse and he helped her up the stairs.

The door to Missy's room stood wide open. He could not see the doctor who stood on the other side of the bed. Missy lay there, propped up on pillows, her hair on her shoulders, her eyes staring.

She saw the crown. He knew at once from the look on her face. The Princess went forward and slowly offered the crown.

From where he stood outside the door Coffin could see only the Princess's back and Missy's face.

He saw Missy's hands appear and reach out and take the crown. Before his fascinated and horrified gaze her hands shakily placed the crown on her head. She couldn't do it properly and it slid askew.

Then Anna shut the door and he walked away. He was glad to be excluded from this scene. But it had given him ideas.

He had thought of the poisonings in domestic terms, thought of Seddon and Miss Barrow, but it wasn't like that at all. This was a murder in a court; it was a palace crime. He ought to have been thinking in terms of the Borgias or something even more remote. He had been living in a Byzantine court.

He heard the door open and close behind him. He turned round in time to see the Princess's face, distorted into an emotion he could not quite recognise. She composed herself as soon as she saw him, and walked towards him firmly. She had the crown again.

"You had better go soon," she said, in a matter of fact way, "unless you wish to meet some old friends. The police will be here soon."

"Is Missy dead?"

"No." She did not add anything to this statement. Together they walked down the stairs and into the yellow salon where the Princess sat down; she avoided the throne. Coffin noticed.

"I've been looking in a crystal ball myself," said Coffin.

"Have you?" She rose, took a key from her pocket, unlocked a cupboard set in the panelling, and took out the green glass ball on its velvet base. "Not this one."

"No." He walked over and looked in. He could only see his own face, all nose. "My own. In my own mind. And I could see some pictures pretty clearly. You were in it, for one."

"It's all in the interpretation," she answered. "The ball distorts. You can't trust what you see, you know that?"

"I'll tell you what I see, you tell me if I can trust it." He went over to the window and looked out. All quiet. He could just imagine how it was going to be in a little while. Police. Television cameras. People standing by and staring.

"I see rivals for a crown. Only a little crown, but a crown. I see money. I certainly see a woman."

"We are all women in this house. You could even include the General. He's an old woman."

"In this crystal ball of mine I see a long planned scheme of murder. The motive was a highly personal one. I agree with you that this poisoner enjoyed the whole process but there was a real selfish motive. Am I seeing the right things?"

She did not deny it.

"You are accusing me. I hear it in your voice."

"You accused yourself."

"I shall never be convicted."

She sat there, looking frail and sick, but her voice was arrogant and proud.

"Don't count on it."

"You forget who I am."

"You might go to prison," he said wearily. "Or hospital, for treatment. There's quite a danger of that, I should think."

She looked down at her hands. The skin was blotchy and pachydermous.

"You're very observant," she said.

"Oh no. Slow. But I saw your hands. Heard your breathing. I wonder someone else hadn't noticed it."

"They were all getting killed off, you see." she said with an unmirthful laugh. "In any case, it is only lately it has got so apparent. I had just begun to notice it myself."

"I'm surprised you did not see the symptoms." He was studying her appearance.

"The peasants back in my country were never affected."

"They were tougher than you. You've been taking regular small doses of arsenic over a long time and you show it. Doses that could either kill you, in the end, or else give you an immunity if you shared a larger dose with someone less protected."

"No one else noticed," said the Princess, holding out her hands.

"Missy did. And Anna too, I think. But Missy had special reason to notice."

He thought about the two old women. Much of an age. They must have grown up together. Had they always hated each other?

"Did you want to kill Missy?"

"Not until this afternoon," said the Princess grimly. "But then I thought: Why not? An eye for an eye and a tooth for a tooth."

"You can say that calmly," he said with admiration.

"We breed good murderers in my family."

"I've already noticed that." He walked to the window again. Still no one there. "Who is Anna?"

He went back to the crystal ball. There was something stirring in the depths now.

"Anna? My sister. Half-sister. Didn't you know?"

"As a matter of fact, I thought she might be your child."

"Me? No." She laughed. "No. When we first came here my father was still alive. Past anything, we thought. But as it turned out, he was not. Somehow he got out into the town." She sighed. "Of course, the Bourbon inheritance is in many ways a very terrible one."

"Does she know?"

"Of course. Everyone knows. There's no mystery."

"Her position is the same as Missy's then?"

"Missy's parents were married morganatically," corrected the Princess. "Of course she could never inherit the Crown, but otherwise…"

"But Missy wanted the Crown, didn't she? I

misunderstood the position here at first. I thought this was a little domestic crime. I didn't realise I was watching a palace revolution. Missy wanted the Crown and all the money that went with it."

"Missy always resented the morganatic marriage," said the Princess softly. "She didn't accept it. She said that the laws of *this* country did not recognise morganatic marriage and therefore, now she lived here, she did not recognise it either."

"So one by one she poisoned off all your old courtiers who could have testified it was only a morganatic union. When they finally were gone it would have been your turn, succumbing to a last big dose and she would have had the crown. And the money contributed by your supporters."

The Princess started to laugh. A tiny tinkling old maid's laugh, but loaded with real amusement.

"What makes it funny?"

"She should have had a word with me. I could have set her straight. My father and Anna's mother were married. But Missy was right: the laws of England regard no marriage as morganatic."

"So you have an heir?"

"But Anna doesn't care. She's going to marry and go away. She doesn't want an out of date old crown that isn't a crown at all." She gave the little crown a push and it fell to the floor.

"Oh, it's a comedy all right." He glanced again towards the window.

"I see you keep looking at the window. The police will be a few minutes yet. I have experience in these things."

"So have I."

"I delayed them a little by giving no address. It will take them a little time to know it is me," she said calmly. "I wanted Missy to die in peace. Also I wanted time to compose myself to make my confession with dignity."

And it was true, with every minute her self-command had strengthened.

"I have to tell them that when I discovered today that Missy had removed one of her secret packets of arsenic I was afraid she was going to kill the General. The General or Anna. Or even, I thought to myself, the lot of us. She has gone on past the point where she knows how to stop, she has a trade now, it is that of poisoner and she loves to practise it."

Coffin nodded. He thought he could at last hear sounds outside.

"So I filled the pot for the camomile tea and I added some arsenic of my own and I challenged Missy to drink it. She knew what she was doing. In the end she wanted to do it. She wasn't frightened."

"Yes, she was. Very frightened."

"Well, who is to say what percentage of fear, pain and pleasure she felt? Who is to say what I feel? I who have been poisoned slowly over the months. I hardly know myself. Do I say thank you, Missy, for putting me nearer my grave?" She stared towards the window. "It has been an experience."

Coffin got up.

"Yes, you'd better go. Before you go, give me the crystal ball."

He handed it to her. As he did so he looked down. He seemed to see a face in it now. Small and dark and bright eyed, it looked like the face of his wife. But she was not alone. He saw another unknown face with hers. Or thought he did.

"I can't go without saying good-bye." He gripped the Princess's hand.

"Good-bye? You haven't seen the last of me yet. They can't touch me, you know. I don't admit their jurisdiction." Her hand went down for the crown again. "I am the source of law and justice here."

"I should ask for a jury of peers, if I were you. They'd have a job rounding up a jury of crowned heads."

"You know where to go, don't you?" she called after him. "You know where to go?"

Yes, he knew where to go.

He was out of the house by the side way, anxious to be gone before the obsequies could begin. In a crystal ball made by Fabergé he had seen his wife's face, and another's. He could swear he had.

He left on foot, walking quickly. But although he was quick he was not quite quick enough. He was seen and recognised by the driver of the police car which was drawn in at the kerb. This man, knowing there was something about Coffin at the moment, but not quite sure what it was, passed on the news to the detective with him and this man, better informed, telephoned the information back.

So before he was well on his way, his superior, Styles, and his wife, Patsy, knew he was coming.

He walked part of the way home briskly and alertly, then caught a bus. The traffic was light for once and he made good speed. He was back in no time at all. Time was rolling backwards. Weeks ago now (but it felt like years) he had left home and it had felt like a long long time to go. Now time was on his side and was running him along. He felt breathless. Otherwise he felt good.

All the stigmata which had afflicted him, wrists, face, seemed to be clearing up. Only the blood on his sleeve remained and that was probably there forever. He realised he was travelling back without luggage of any sort. Somehow on the way he had lost it all. However you can never really turn back empty-handed. You always bring something back with you.

At the corner of his own road, by the big tree, a car was drawn up and as he passed a familiar figure got out.

"Oh, it's you," he said in surprise.

"Didn't expect me?"

"It's not your usual place."

"Not yours," said Styles.

"I haven't had one lately."

"Noo." He made the noise a long one. "We were watching you. We had our eye on you."

"What?"

"Yes. Did you think you were lost, boy?" he said, in a soft voice. "We knew where you were all the time."

"I wanted to be on my own."

"That's dangerous work," observed Styles, mildly.

"It'll soon be over now. I'll be back at work next week."

"Not before you're ready."

"I'm ready."

"I'll be glad to have you back." He seemed reassured by what he had seen. "Funny stories you hear, don't you, not all of them true. We've got to the bottom of the Spicerman Street business. It was the man Kedge. He wanted to marry the girl. Imprisoned her by way of a courtship. 'Fraid she'd get away, I suppose. So she would have. So he killed her instead. A nut case, boy."

"Poor kid."

"Which one?"

"Both of them."

"I'm on the side of the victim," said Styles, firmly and resolutely.

"So am I. Provided you can find out which is which."

"That's not your job."

"Not in the past," said Coffin thoughtfully. "No."

His wife came running, tumbling to open the door as soon as she realised it was him.

"I knew it was you."

"Styles phoned you, I suppose," said Coffin, taking off his coat. The bloodstain went with it. "He seems to have been keeping a check on me."

"You did behave oddly." She looked anxious.

"I know it."

She still looked anxious, but came nearer.

"Are you staying long or just looking in?" she asked cautiously.

"That depends. Partly on me. Partly on you. On how you feel about the man in Philadelphia. Or was it Pittsburgh?"

"Pittsburgh," she said. "How did you know about that?"

"I saw it in a crystal ball. Anyway, I saw you both."

"I think you only see in a crystal ball what you know already."

"I didn't expect to see his face," complained her husband.

"That old woman's a witch. And in any case, that isn't why you went, and what you saw in a crystal ball isn't why you came back."

"No."

"You just wanted to run."

"Well, I'll tell you how it was. I thought I would go away and find out what a *good* person I was. Too good for my job. That's what I thought I'd find."

"And did you?"

"No. Just the opposite."

"You should have asked me," said his wife.

They both began to laugh. When things are as bad as they have seemed to be and you know it, a laugh is about the only thing to offer.

"You want to take yourself in hand."

"I've begun," said Coffin. "I've started."

"I've been frightened of you," she said, watching. "And yet, I didn't believe you would really hurt me. You didn't, did you?"

"I did want to, though. Well sort of. No, perhaps that isn't really what I wanted."

They stood staring at each other.

"I thought you came back once and walked inside the house. I thought I saw signs inside the house next morning."

He shook his head. "No, never. That was your imagination."

He walked up the stairs into their living room. She followed.

"I did try one night. But I couldn't get in."

"I think I heard you." She had sat here on the stairs and listened. She could remember it and so later would he. It was going to be a hard thing to absorb into their past. Nothing had been solved by his going away, but a lot of new things had been started.

"Why couldn't I get in? What was wrong with my key?"

"I had the locks changed."

Here was another fact you couldn't save as a story to tell your grandchildren. You could have a lover in Pittsburgh and locks on the door and you had to take it as part of your world. No pretending someone else made it for you.

"Do you know, it nearly made me think I'd done a murder," said Coffin. "That's how far I was gone."

The telephone rang. He reached for it and answered it.

"Hello?" It was Alberta.

"You always know how to find me," he exclaimed. He could see his wife raise her eyebrows and he took her hand and held it.

"But of course. I told you so. There's a link between you and me. But I rang to tell you that it's all right about the boy. He won't die."

"And Jess?"

"She's gone home. I've settled everything."

"You drive too hard a bargain."

"I was pleased with the work you did for me," said Alberta. "There'll be more work for you. I'll keep in touch. I shall know where to find you." She finished the call.

He put the telephone down.

"I think I need a crystal ball of my own," said his wife.

"Who was that?"

"A goddess," said Coffin. "Or a saint."

"A goddess and a princess," mocked his wife. "What company you've been keeping."

"I'm going to find out about Alberta," said Coffin, springing to his feet. "She comes from Wales. She didn't like me knowing that. There's a story there and I'd like to know it."

Going away hadn't solved anything, hadn't made anything any better, there was nothing to do now but pick it up where he had left it with a few extra burdens added on. But he still kept hold of his wife's hand.

"I'll just go up to my room and settle in." He had a small workroom upstairs and it was where he always went first after coming home. It was a normal gesture, what he had always done.

He went upstairs, opened the door and looked around. Things had been moved, and drawers on the desk were open, books were on the floor.

"You been in here?" he called back to his wife.

"No, not lately." She came to look.

"Then you were right. Someone has been in this house. There was someone here that night you thought there was. You weren't imagining."

Coffin did not know anything about Edward Arnold Jones, the man without a name, but he was on the alert.

One night the man without a name had got inside Coffin's house and moved cautiously around one room. He had heard Patsy Coffin go down the stairs and debated momentarily whether he should go for her and decided against it. If she left him alone, he would leave her alone. Besides, he really preferred older women. Much much older. His last victim had been about fifty and respectably married, but she still hadn't complained to the police. In any case it was Coffin himself he wanted.

"I'll be back," he said aloud. "I'll get away now. But I'll be back." In his pocket he had the key to Coffin's house which he had procured in a manner all his own. "I'll wait for him to come home then I'll call again."

Coffin started to pick up his books and tidy the desk.

"It never stops, does it? It seems as if there was one great burst of violence that goes on and on producing more violence all the time. It's never going to end. It'll be round us all the time."

Prowling about outside the house, Edward Arnold Jones had already noticed that Coffin was back and was debating what to do about it. He still had the key to the house. One he had stolen from the purse of the new daily cleaning woman whom Patsy alternately indulged and overworked. She was the latest of his victims. Another thing Coffin did not know was this woman's continuing relationship with Jones. He had a spy now in his own house.

But in spite of his words Coffin no longer felt helpless. The violence is there, he was thinking, inside me, inside you, and it's going to come out, but I can do something to control it.

"Someone's got a key to this house," he said, looking at his wife. "And I'm going to find out who it is."

GWENDOLINE BUTLER

COFFIN IN OXFORD

"It was like a Chinese puzzle. In St Ebbe's was a flat, in the flat was a trunk, and in the trunk was a body. The body of a woman..."

Ted was brought round from the first attack, if you could call it an attack, with difficulty. He had been found shut up in a cupboard with a scarf tightened around his neck: his own scarf, to add insult to injury...

THIS IS THE FIRST TIME in paperback for this novel featuring Gwendoline Butler's popular sleuth, John Coffin. The fact that Gwendoline Butler is one of the most borrowed authors in Britain will come as no surprise to her many readers. She is also one of the most universally praised, and with good reason. Recently voted one of the world's Top 200 crime writers, If you haven't tried Gwendoline Butler, why not start now?

'Gwendoline Butler is excellent on the bizarre fantasies of other people's lives and on modern paranoia overlaying old secrets; and her plots have the rare ability to shock'

—ANDREW TAYLOR, THE INDEPENDENT

Price: £4.99 ISBN: 1-902002-00-8

Available from all good bookshops, or post free from: CT Publishing, PO Box 5880, Birmingham B16 8JF

email ct@crimetime.demon.co.uk

CT PUBLISHING

If you have enjoyed this title we feel sure you will enjoy these other titles from us:

Coffin in Oxford	Gwendoline Butler	1902002008	£4.99
A Nameless Coffin	Gwendoline Butler	1902002113	£4.99
Coffin Following	Gwendoline Butler	1902002105	£4.99
Cage of Night	Ed Gorman	1902002024	£4.99
Night Kills	Ed Gorman	1902002032	£4.99
Poker Club [H/B]	Ed Gorman	1902002075	£16.99
The Long Midnight	Ed Gorman	1902002083	£4.99
Serpents Kiss	Ed Gorman	1902002091	£4.99
Windsor Red	Jennie Melville	1902002016	£4.99
Singleminded	Hélène de monagahan	190200213x	£6.99

They are available from all good bookshops, or post free from:

CT Publishing, (Dept GB3) PO Box 5880, Edgbaston, Birmingham B16 8JF

or you can order via our web site at:

www.crimetime.co.uk

email **ct@crimetime.demon.co.uk**

DO *YOU* HAVE TIME FOR CRIME...?

CRIME TIME

IF YOU HAVE ENJOYED this book you may like to try our quarterly round-up of all that's best in the world of crime fiction. Now in its third year, CRIME TIME is acknowledged as the best publication about crime fiction in the world. Interviews, features and reviews mingle with new fiction by some of the world's best writers in a 256 page plus trade paperback format for only £4.99 for a sample copy or £20 for a year's subscription, plus a free book.

Recent interviewees and contributors include Ed Gorman, Michelle Spring, Colin Dexter, Mark Timlin, Gwendoline Butler, James Ellroy, Elizabeth George, James Sallis, Patricia Cornwell, Jonathan and Faye Kellerman, Ben Elton, Andrew Klavan, Lauren Henderson, Maxim Jakubowski, Ed McBain, James Patterson, Lawrence Block, Joe R Lansdale and many more.

In addition we have run features, often exclusives, such as Derek Raymond on Ted Lewis, Mike Hodges on making *Get Carter*, a history of Hardboiled fiction, Criminal Cities, featured TV shows such as *Homicide* (with cast interviews) and *The Sweeney*, as well as covering film, radio, audio tapes, video, comics and the theatre.

Why not join in? More reading than the telephone directory of a small town and much more interesting...

Price: £2.99 for a sample issue /
£20 for 4 issues + free book
Available from all good bookshops, or post free from:
CT Publishing, (Dept GB2) PO Box 5880, Birmingham B16 8JF
email ct@crimetime.demon.co.uk